DIANA WYNNE JONES

BELIEVING IS SEEING

SEVEN STORIES

WITH ILLUSTRATIONS BY
NENAD JAKESEVIC

Greenwillow Books, New York

Library of Congress Cataloging-in-Publication Data
Jones, Diana Wynne.
Believing is seeing : seven stories / by Diana Wynne Jones.
p.   cm.
Contents: The sage of Theare—The master—Enna Hittims—
The girl who loved the sun—Dragon reserve, home eight—
What the cat told me—nad and Dan adn Quaffy.
ISBN 0-688-16843-4
1. Fantasy fiction, English.   2. Children's stories, English.
[1. Fantasy.   2. Short stories.]   1. Title.   PZ7.J684Se   1999
[Fic]—dc21   98-41805   CIP   AC

CONTENTS

INTRODUCTION

These stories were written at intervals over a long period, and it so happened that each time I had written one of them, someone asked me for a story for a collection. I began to feel positively precognitive.

The trouble is that the collection didn't always match the story. "The Sage of Theare" started because I remembered, or thought I remembered, a story by Borges being read on the radio, in which a scholar arduously tracked down a learned man but never quite found him. I have never actually found that story either. If it exists, it behaves like its own plot. But years after I thought I remembered hearing it, I started having dreams about it—strange circular dreams in a strange city where gods took a hand—and the dream person never found the wise man he was looking for. In order to exorcise the dreams, I wrote the story. I was writing Chrestomanci books at the time, so the story fairly naturally included Chrestomanci, too. While I was finishing it, Susan Schwartz asked me for something for a collection called *Hecate's Cauldron*, and with some doubts, I sent it to her. She used it, and to my dismay, it stuck out like a sore thumb. All the other stories were very female. Chrestomanci strides among them like a grasshopper in a beehive. His effect on the gods in the story is rather the same, too.

"The Master" was another dream, or maybe a nightmare, which I dreamed more than once and had again to exorcise by writing it down. I know it is really part of the complex of ideas out of which *Fire and Hemlock* got written, but I couldn't explain how. It is, of course, about precognition. At that time, I was quite worried about the way most of my books came true at me after I had written them, but I am glad to say that the events in "The Master" have (so far) not happened to me.

One rainy afternoon quite a long time later I sat down and wrote "The Girl Who Loved the Sun." I had been thinking about all those Greek stories where women get turned into plants and animals, and I kept wondering *how* and *why: how* it felt to the person it happened to and *why* they let it happen. It seemed to me that nothing that radical could happen to someone without their personal consent, and I wondered *why* one might consent. When I had done the first draft, I had two phone calls. The first was from my sister, who wanted to tell me she had been writing poems about women who were turned into plants and animals and asking much the same questions as I had (my sister and I seem to share trains of thought quite often), and the second was someone wanting a story about unhappy love. I sent this story, as doubtfully as I had earlier sent "The Sage of Theare," because I was not sure it quite counted. But they said it did. You must see what you think.

Peculiarly, I do not remember why I wrote "Enna Hittims," but I presume I was sick in bed and feeling bored. And when Greenwillow asked me for a new story for this collection, it was ready and waiting.

Much earlier than all of these, while I was thinking out the multiplicity of alternate worlds that occur in *The Lives of Christopher Chant,* I wrote "Dragon Reserve, Home Eight" almost by way of clarifying things. At that time, though, I was thinking of the worlds as rather like a wad of different colored paper handkerchiefs. If you were to take that wad and crumple it in one hand, each color would be separate, but wrapped in with the others. And I was also thinking of an enchanter's gifts rather more as inborn psychic talents. As so often happens, when I came to write the actual book a good four years later, everything turned out differently, and probably no one would realize this story had anything to do with it unless I told them. Again, I had just done a rather rough and unsatisfactory first draft when Robin McKinley asked me for a fantasy story. I sent this one, but she refused it on the grounds that it was not fantasy. This struck me as fair and reasonable, even though I knew it was going to be fantasy later.

I asked myself for a story with "What the Cat Told Me." When I wrote it, I was suffering cat deprivation. I was brought up with cats and didn't have one at that time (this was four years ago, just before someone suddenly arrived and organized me a cat, so this one came true in a way). I love the exacting self-centeredness of cats. The story is about that. Then I was asked to compile a collection of fantasy stories, and I put this one in among the original selection, which I knew was going to be far too long. I mean, what can one *leave out* of a fantasy collection? My idea was to leave my own story out. But when it came to cutting the list down to publishable size, the editors, to my great surprise, insisted that this one stay in. I was glad. It was fun to write.

It was even more fun to write "nad and Dan adn Quaffy." This one is a loving send-up of a well-known author whose writing I admire and read so avidly that I'm sure I know where a lot of it comes from. The idea for it came to me as I typed *nad* for *and* for the hundredth time, changed it, found it was now *adn*, reached for my coffee in frustration, and idly realized—among other things—that this other writer did this, too. Typos are a great inspiration. Depending on which side you hit the wrong key, *coffee* can be either *xiddaw* or *voggrr*, both of which are obviously alien substances that induce a state of altered consciousness. And yet again, when I was halfway through it, giggling as I wrote, I was asked for a story about computers.

And there you are: believing is seeing.

Diana Wynne Jones
Bristol, 1999

THE SAGE
OF THEARE

There was a world called Theare in which Heaven was very well organized. Everything was so precisely worked out that every god knew his or her exact duties, correct prayers, right times for business, utterly exact character, and unmistakable place above or below other gods. This was the case from Great Zond, the king of the gods, through every god, godlet, deity, minor deity, and numen, down to the most immaterial nymph. Even the invisible dragons that lived in the rivers had their invisible lines of demarcation. The universe ran like clockwork. Mankind was not always so regular, but the gods were there to set him right. It had been like this for centuries.

So it was a breach in the very nature of things when, in the middle of the yearly Festival of Water, at which only watery deities were entitled to be present, Great Zond looked up to see Imperion, god of the sun, storming toward him down the halls of Heaven.

"Go away!" cried Zond, aghast.

But Imperion swept on, causing the watery deities gathered there to steam and hiss, and arrived in a wave of heat and warm water at the foot of Zond's high throne.

"Father!" Imperion cried urgently.

A high god like Imperion was entitled to call Zond Father. Zond did not recall whether or not he was actually Imperion's father. The origins of the gods were not quite so orderly as their present existence. But Zond knew that, son of his or not, Imperion had breached all the rules. "Abase yourself," Zond said sternly.

Imperion ignored this command, too. Perhaps this was just as well, since the floor of Heaven was awash already, and steaming. Imperion kept his flaming gaze on Zond. "Father! The Sage of Dissolution has been born!"

Zond shuddered in the clouds of hot vapor and tried to feel resigned. "It is written," he said, "a Sage shall be born who shall question everything. His questions shall bring down the exquisite order of Heaven and cast all the gods into disorder. It is also written—" Here Zond realized that Imperion had made him break the rules, too. The correct procedure was for Zond to summon the god of prophecy and have that god consult the Book of Heaven. Then he realized that Imperion *was* the god of prophecy. It was one of his precisely allocated duties. Zond rounded on Imperion. "What do you mean coming and telling me? You're god of prophecy! Go and look in the Book of Heaven!"

"I already have, Father," said Imperion. "I find I prophesied the coming of the Sage of Dissolution when the gods first began. It is written that the Sage shall be born and that I shall not know."

"Then," said Zond, scoring a point, "how is it you're here telling me he *has* been born?"

"The mere fact," Imperion said, "that I can come here and interrupt the Water Festival shows that the Sage has been born. Our Dissolution has obviously begun."

There was a splash of consternation among the watery gods. They were gathered down the hall as far as they could get from Imperion, but they had all heard. Zond tried to gather his wits. What with the steam raised by Imperion and the spume of dismay thrown out by the rest, the halls of Heaven were in a state nearer chaos than he had known for millennia. Any more of this, and there would be no need for the Sage to ask questions. "Leave us," Zond said to the watery gods. "Events even beyond my control cause this festival to be stopped. You will be informed later of any decision I make." To Zond's dismay, the watery ones hesitated—further evidence of Dissolution. "I promise," he said.

The watery ones made up their minds. They left in waves, all except one. This one was Ock, god of all oceans. Ock was equal in status to Imperion, and heat did not threaten him. He stayed where he was.

Zond was not pleased. Ock, it always seemed to him, was the least orderly of the gods. He did not know his place. He was as restless and unfathomable as mankind. But, with Dissolution already begun, what could Zond do? "You have our permission to stay," he said graciously to Ock, and to Imperion: "Well, how did you know the Sage was born?"

"I was consulting the Book of Heaven on another matter," said Imperion, "and the page opened at my prophecy concerning the Sage of Dissolution. Since it said that I would not know the day and hour when the Sage was born, it followed that he has already been born, or I would not have known. The rest of the prophecy was commendably precise, however. Twenty years from now, he will start questioning Heaven. What shall we do to stop him?"

"I don't see what we can do," Zond said hopelessly. "A prophecy is a prophecy."

"But we must do something!" brazed Imperion. "I insist! I am a god of order, even more than you are. Think what would happen if the sun went inaccurate! This means more to me than anyone. I want the Sage of Dissolution found and killed before he can ask questions."

Zond was shocked. "I can't do that! If the prophecy says he has to ask questions, then he has to ask them."

Here Ock approached. "Every prophecy has a loophole," he said.

"Of course," snapped Imperion. "I can see the loophole as well as you. I'm taking advantage of the disorder caused by the birth of the Sage to ask Great Zond to kill him and overthrow the prophecy. Thus restoring order."

"Logic chopping is not what I meant," said Ock.

The two gods faced one another. Steam from Ock suffused Imperion and then rained back on Ock, as regularly as breathing. "What did you mean, then?" said Imperion.

"The prophecy," said Ock, "does not appear to say which world the Sage will ask his questions in. There are many other worlds. Mankind calls them if-worlds, meaning that they were once the same world as Theare, but split off and went their own ways after each doubtful event in history. Each if-world has its own Heaven. There must be one world in which the gods are not as orderly as we are here. Let the Sage be put in that world. Let him ask his predestined questions there."

"Good idea!" Zond clapped his hands in relief, causing untoward tempests in all Theare. "Agreed, Imperion?"

"Yes," said Imperion. He flamed with relief. And being unguarded, he at once became prophetic. "But I must warn you," he said, "that strange things happen when destiny is tampered with."

"Strange things maybe, but never disorderly," Zond asserted. He called the watery gods back and, with them, every god in Theare. He told them that an infant had just been born who was destined to spread Dissolution, and he ordered each one of them to search the ends of the earth for this child. ("The ends of the earth" was a legal formula. Zond did not believe that Theare was flat. But the expression had been unchanged for centuries, just like the rest of Heaven. It meant "Look everywhere.")

The whole of Heaven looked high and low. Nymphs and god-lets scanned mountains, caves, and woods. Household gods peered into cradles. Watery gods searched beaches, banks, and margins. The goddess of love went deeply into her records, to find who the Sage's parents might be. The invisible dragons swam to look inside barges and houseboats. Since there was a god for everything in Theare, nowhere was missed, nothing was omitted. Imperion searched harder than any, blazing into every nook and crevice on one side of the world, and exhorting the moon goddess to do the same on the other side.

And nobody found the Sage. There were one or two false alarms, such as when a household goddess reported an infant that never stopped crying. This baby, she said, was driving her up the wall, and if this was not Dissolution, she would like to know what was. There were also several reports of infants born with teeth, or six fingers, or suchlike strangeness. But in each case Zond was able to prove that the child had nothing to do with Dissolution. After a month it became clear that the infant Sage was not going to be found.

Imperion was in despair, for as he had told Zond, order meant more to him than to any other god. He became so worried that he was actually causing the sun to lose heat. At length the goddess of love advised him to go off and relax with a mortal woman before he brought about Dissolution himself. Imperion saw she was right. He went down to visit the human woman he had loved for some years. It was established custom for gods to love mortals. Some visited their loves in all sorts of fanciful shapes, and some had many loves at once. But Imperion was both honest and faithful. He never visited Nestara as anything but a handsome man, and he loved her devotedly. Three years ago she had borne him a son, whom Imperion loved almost as much as he loved Nestara. Before the Sage was born to trouble him, Imperion had been trying to bend the rules of Heaven a little, to get his son approved as a god, too.

The child's name was Thasper. As Imperion descended to earth, he could see Thasper digging in some sand outside Nestara's house—a beautiful child, fair-haired and blue-eyed. Imperion wondered fondly if Thasper was talking properly yet. Nestara had been worried about how slowly he was learning to speak.

Imperion alighted beside his son. "Hello, Thasper. What are you digging so busily?"

Instead of answering, Thasper raised his golden head and shouted. "Mum!" he yelled. "Why does it go bright when Dad comes?"

All Imperion's pleasure vanished. Of course no one could ask questions until he had learned to speak. But it would be too cruel if his own son turned out to be the Sage of Dissolution. "Why shouldn't it go bright?" he asked defensively.

Thasper scowled up at him. "I want to know. *Why* does it?"

"Perhaps because you feel happy to see me," Imperion suggested.

"I'm not happy," Thasper said. His lower lip came out. Tears filled his big blue eyes. "Why does it go bright? I want to *know*. Mum! I'm not happy!"

Nestara came racing out of the house, almost too concerned to smile at Imperion. "Thasper love, what's the matter?"

"I want to *know*!" wailed Thasper.

"What do you want to know? I've never known such an inquiring mind," Nestara said proudly to Imperion as she picked Thasper up. "That's why he was so slow talking. He wouldn't speak until he'd found out how to ask questions. And if you don't give him an exact answer, he'll cry for hours."

"When did he first start asking questions?" Imperion inquired tensely.

"About a month ago," said Nestara.

This made Imperion truly miserable, but he concealed it. It

was clear to him that Thasper was indeed the Sage of Dissolution and he was going to have to take him away to another world. He smiled and said, "My love, I have wonderful news for you. Thasper has been accepted as a god. Great Zond himself will have him as cupbearer."

"Oh, not now!" cried Nestara. "He's so little!"

She made numerous other objections, too. But in the end she let Imperion take Thasper. After all, what better future could there be for a child? She put Thasper into Imperion's arms with all sorts of anxious advice about what he ate and when he went to bed. Imperion kissed her good-bye, heavy-hearted. He was not a god of deception. He knew he dared not see her again for fear he told her the truth.

Then, with Thasper in his arms, Imperion went up to the middle regions below Heaven, to look for another world.

Thasper looked down with interest at the great blue curve of the world. "Why—" he began.

Imperion hastily enclosed him in a sphere of forgetfulness. He could not afford to let Thasper ask things here. Questions that spread Dissolution on earth would have an even more powerful effect in the middle region. The sphere was a silver globe, neither transparent nor opaque. In it, Thasper would stay seemingly asleep, not moving and not growing, until the sphere was opened. With the child thus safe, Imperion hung the sphere from one shoulder and stepped into the next-door world.

He went from world to world. He was pleased to find there was an almost infinite number of them, for the choice proved supremely difficult. Some worlds were so disorderly that he shrank from leaving Thasper in them. In some, the gods resented Imperion's intrusion and shouted at him to be off. In others, it was mankind that was resentful. One world he came to was so rational that to his horror, he found the gods were dead. There were many others he thought might do, until he let the spirit of prophecy blow through him, and in each case this told him that harm would come to Thasper here. But at last he found a good world. It seemed calm and elegant. The few gods there seemed civilized but casual. Indeed, Imperion was a little puzzled to find that these gods seemed to share quite a lot of their power with mankind. But mankind did not seem to abuse this power, and the spirit of prophecy assured him that, if he left Thasper here inside his sphere of forgetfulness, it would be opened by someone who would treat the boy well.

Imperion put the sphere down in a wood and sped back to Theare, heartily relieved. There he reported what he had done to Zond, and all Heaven rejoiced. Imperion made sure that Nestara married a very rich man who gave her not only wealth and happiness but plenty of children to replace Thasper. Then, a little sadly, he went back to the ordered life of Heaven. The exquisite organization of Theare went on untroubled by Dissolution.

Seven years passed.

All that while Thasper knew nothing and remained three years old. Then, one day, the sphere of forgetfulness fell in two halves, and he blinked in sunlight somewhat less golden than he had known.

"So that's what was causing all the disturbance," a tall man murmured.

"Poor little soul!" said a lady.

There was a wood around Thasper, and people standing in it looking at him, but, as far as Thasper knew, nothing had happened since he soared to the middle region with his father. He went on with the question he had been in the middle of asking. "Why is the world round?" he said.

"Interesting question," said the tall man. "The answer usually given is because the corners wore off spinning around the sun. But it could be designed to make us end where we began."

"Sir, you'll muddle him, talking like that," said another lady. "He's only little."

"No, he's interested," said another man. "Look at him."

Thasper was indeed interested. He approved of the tall man. He was a little puzzled about where he had come from, but he supposed the tall man must have been put there because he answered questions better than Imperion. He wondered where Imperion had got to. "Why aren't you my dad?" he asked the tall man.

"Another most penetrating question," said the tall man. "Because, as far as we can find out, your father lives in another world. Tell me your name."

This was another point in the tall man's favor. Thasper never answered questions; he only asked them. But this was a command. The tall man understood Thasper. "Thasper," Thasper answered obediently.

"He's sweet!" said the first lady. "I want to adopt him." To which the other ladies gathered around most heartily agreed.

"Impossible," said the tall man. His tone was mild as milk and rock firm. The ladies were reduced to begging to be able to look after Thasper for a day then. An hour. "No," the tall man said mildly. "He must go back at once." At which all the ladies cried out that Thasper might be in great danger in his own home. The tall man said, "I shall take care of that, of course." Then he stretched out a hand and pulled Thasper up. "Come along, Thasper."

As soon as Thasper was out of it, the two halves of the sphere vanished. One of the ladies took his other hand, and he was led away, first on a jiggly ride, which he much enjoyed, and then into a huge house, where there was a very perplexing room. In this room Thasper sat in a five-pointed star and pictures kept appearing around him. People kept shaking their heads. "No, not that world either." The tall man answered all Thasper's questions, and Thasper was too interested even to be annoyed when they would not allow him anything to eat.

"Why not?" he said.

"Because, just by being here, you are causing the world to jolt about," the tall man explained. "If you put food inside you, food is a heavy part of this world, and it might jolt you to pieces."

Soon after that a new picture appeared. Everyone said "Ah!" and the tall man said, "So it's Theare!" He looked at Thasper in a surprised way. "You must have struck someone as disorderly," he said. Then he looked at the picture again, in a lazy, careful kind of way. "No disorder," he said. "No danger. Come with me."

He took Thasper's hand again and led him into the picture. As he did so, Thasper's hair turned much darker. "A simple precaution," the tall man murmured, a little apologetically, but Thasper did not even notice. He was not aware what color his hair had been to start with, and besides, he was taken up with surprise at how fast they were going. They whizzed into a city and stopped abruptly. It was a good house, just on the edge of a poorer district. "Here is someone who will do," the tall man said, and he knocked at the door.

A sad-looking lady opened the door.

"I beg your pardon, madam," said the tall man. "Have you by any chance lost a small boy?"

"Yes," said the lady. "But this isn't—" She blinked, "Yes, it is!" she cried out. "Oh, Thasper! How could you run off like that? Thank you so much, sir." But the tall man had gone.

The lady's name was Alina Altun, and she was so convinced that she was Thasper's mother that Thasper was soon convinced, too. He settled in happily with her and her husband, who was a doctor, hardworking but not very rich. Thasper soon forgot the tall man, Imperion, and Nestara. Sometimes it did puzzle him—

and his new mother, too—that when she showed him off to her friends, she always felt bound to say, "This is Badien, but we always call him Thasper." Thanks to the tall man, none of them ever knew that the real Badien had wandered away the day Thasper came, and fell in the river, where an invisible dragon ate him.

If Thasper had remembered the tall man, he might also have wondered why his arrival seemed to start Dr. Altun on the road to prosperity. The people in the poorer district nearby suddenly discovered what a good doctor Dr. Altun was, and how little he charged. Alina was shortly able to afford to send Thasper to a very good school, where Thasper often exasperated his teachers by his many questions. He had, as his new mother often proudly said, a most inquiring mind. Although he learned quicker than most the Ten First Lessons and the Nine Graces of Childhood, his teachers were nevertheless often annoyed enough to snap, "Oh, go and ask an invisible dragon!" which is what people in Theare often said when they thought they were being pestered.

Thasper did, with difficulty, gradually cure himself of his habit of never answering questions. But he always preferred asking to answering. At home he asked questions all the time: "Why does the kitchen god go and report to Heaven once a year? Is it so I can steal biscuits? Why are there invisible dragons? Is there a god for everything? Why is there a god for everything? If the gods make people ill, how can Dad cure them? Why must I have a baby brother or sister?"

Alina Altun was a good mother. She most diligently answered all these questions, including the last. She told Thasper how babies were made, ending her account with, "Then, if the gods bless my womb, a baby will come." She was a devout person.

"I don't want you to be blessed!" Thasper said, resorting to a statement, which he only did when he was strongly moved.

He seemed to have no choice in the matter. By the time he

was ten years old, the gods had thought fit to bless him with two brothers and two sisters. In Thasper's opinion, they were, as blessings, very low grade. They were just too young to be any use. "Why can't they be the same age as me?" he demanded, many times. He began to bear the gods a small but definite grudge about this.

Dr. Altun continued to prosper, and his earnings more than kept pace with his family. Alina employed a nursemaid, a cook, and a number of rather impermanent houseboys. It was one of these houseboys who, when Thasper was eleven, shyly presented Thasper with a folded square of paper. Wondering, Thasper unfolded it. It gave him a curious feeling to touch, as if the paper was vibrating a little in his fingers. It also gave out a very strong warning that he was not to mention it to anybody. It said:

> Dear Thasper,
>   Your situation is an odd one. Make sure that you
> call me at the moment when you come face to face
> with yourself. I shall be watching and I will come at
> once.
>   Yrs,
>   Chrestomanci

Since Thasper by now had not the slightest recollection of his early life, this letter puzzled him extremely. He knew he was not supposed to tell anyone about it, but he also knew that this did not include the houseboy. With the letter in his hand, he hurried after the houseboy to the kitchen.

He was stopped at the head of the kitchen stairs by a tremendous smashing of china from below. This was followed immediately by the cook's voice raised in nonstop abuse. Thasper knew it was no good trying to go into the kitchen. The houseboy—who went by the odd name of Cat—was in the process of getting fired, like all the other houseboys before him. He had better go and wait for Cat outside the back door. Thasper looked at the letter in his hand. As he did so, his fingers tingled. The letter vanished.

"It's gone!" he exclaimed, showing by this statement how astonished he was. He never could account for what he did next. Instead of going to wait for the houseboy, he ran to the living room, intending to tell his mother about it, in spite of the warning. "Do you know what?" he began. He had invented this meaningless question so that he could tell people things and still make it into an inquiry. "Do you know what?" Alina looked up. Thasper, though he fully intended to tell her about the mysterious letter, found himself saying, "The cook's just sacked the new houseboy."

"Oh, bother!" said Alina. "I shall have to find another one now."

Annoyed with himself, Thasper tried to tell her again. "Do you know what? I'm surprised the cook doesn't sack the kitchen god, too."

"Hush, dear. Don't talk about the gods that way!" said the devout lady.

By this time the houseboy had left and Thasper lost the urge to tell anyone about the letter. It remained with him as his own personal exciting secret. He thought of it as the Letter from a Person Unknown. He sometimes whispered the strange name of the Person Unknown to himself when no one could hear. But nothing ever happened, even when he said the name out loud. He gave up doing that after a while. He had other things to think about. He became fascinated by Rules, Laws, and Systems.

Rules and Systems were an important part of the life of mankind in Theare. It stood to reason, with Heaven so well organized. People codified all behavior into things like the Seven Subtle Politenesses or the Hundred Roads to Godliness. Thasper had been taught these things from the time he was three years old. He was accustomed to hearing Alina argue the niceties of the Seventy-two Household Laws with her friends. Now Thasper suddenly discovered for himself that all Rules made a magnificent framework for one's mind to clamber about in. He made lists of rules, and refinements on rules, and possible ways of doing the opposite of what the rules said while still keeping the rules. He invented new codes of rules. He filled books and made charts. He invented games with huge and complicated rules and played them with his friends. Onlookers found these games both rough and muddled, but Thasper and his friends reveled in them. The best moment in any game was when somebody stopped playing and shouted, "I've thought of a new rule!"

This obsession with rules lasted until Thasper was fifteen. He was walking home from school one day, thinking over a list of rules for Twenty Fashionable Hairstyles. From this it will be seen that Thasper was noticing girls, though none of the girls had so far seemed to notice him. And he was thinking which girl should wear which hairstyle when his attention was caught by words chalked on a wall:

> IF RULES MAKE A FRAMEWORK FOR THE MIND TO
> CLIMB ABOUT IN, WHY SHOULD THE MIND NOT
> CLIMB RIGHT OUT? SAYS THE SAGE OF DISSOLUTION.

That same day, there was consternation again in Heaven. Zond summoned all the high gods to his throne. "The Sage of Dissolution has started to preach," he announced direfully. "Imperion, I thought you got rid of him."

"I thought I did," Imperion said. He was even more appalled than Zond. If the Sage had started to preach, it meant that Imperion had got rid of Thasper and deprived himself of Nestara quite unnecessarily. "I must have been mistaken," he admitted.

Here Ock spoke up, steaming gently. "Father Zond," he said,

"may I respectfully suggest that you deal with the Sage yourself, so that there will be no mistake this time?"

"That was just what I was about to suggest," Zond said gratefully. "Are you all agreed?"

All the gods agreed. They were too used to order to do otherwise.

As for Thasper, he was staring at the chalked words, shivering to the soles of his sandals. What was this? Who was using his own private thoughts about rules? Who was this Sage of Dissolution? Thasper was ashamed. He, who was so good at asking questions, had never thought of asking this one. Why should one's mind not climb right out of the rules, after all?

He went home and asked his parents about the Sage of Dissolution. He fully expected them to know. He was quite agitated when they did not. But they had a neighbor, who sent Thasper to another neighbor, who had a friend, who, when Thasper finally found his house, said he had heard that the Sage was a clever young man who made a living by mocking the gods.

The next day someone had washed the words off. But the day after that a badly printed poster appeared on the same wall.

THE SAGE OF DISSOLUTION ASKS BY WHOSE ORDER IS
ORDER ANYWAY?? COME TO SMALL UNCTION SUBLIME
CONCERT HALL TONIGHT 6:30.

At 6:20 Thasper was having supper. At 6:24 he made up his mind and left the table. At 6:32 he arrived panting at Small Unction Hall. It proved to be a small shabby building quite near where he lived. Nobody was there. As far as Thasper could gather from the grumpy caretaker, the meeting had been the night before. Thasper turned away, deeply disappointed. Who ordered the order was a question he now longed to know the answer to. It was deep. He had a notion that the man who called himself the Sage of Dissolution was truly brilliant.

By way of feeding his own disappointment, he went to school

the next day by a route which took him past the Small Unction Concert Hall. It had burned down in the night. There were only blackened brick walls left. When he got to school, a number of people were talking about it. They said it had burst into flames just before seven the night before.

"Did you know," Thasper said, "that the Sage of Dissolution was there the day before yesterday?"

That was how he discovered he was not the only one interested in the Sage. Half his class were admirers of Dissolution. That, too, was when the girls deigned to notice him. "He's amazing about the gods," one girl told him. "No one ever asked questions like that before." Most of the class, however, girls and boys alike, only knew a little more than Thasper, and most of what they knew was secondhand. But a boy showed him a carefully cut-out newspaper article in which a well-known scholar discussed what he called "the so-called Doctrine of Dissolution." It said, long-windedly, that the Sage and his followers were rude to the gods and against all the rules. It did not tell Thasper much, but it was something. He saw, rather ruefully, that his obsession with rules had been quite wrongheaded and had, into the bargain, caused him to fall behind the rest of his class in learning of this wonderful new doctrine. He became a Disciple of Dissolution on the spot. He joined the rest of his class in finding out all they could about the Sage. He went around with them, writing up on walls:

DISSOLUTION RULES OK.

For a long while after that, the only thing any of Thasper's class could learn of the Sage were scraps of questions chalked on walls and quickly rubbed out.

WHAT NEED OF PRAYER? WHY SHOULD THERE BE A
HUNDRED ROADS TO GODLINESS, NOT MORE OR LESS?
DO WE CLIMB ANYWHERE ON THE STEPS TO HEAVEN?

WHAT IS PERFECTION: A PROCESS OR A STATE? WHEN WE
CLIMB TO PERFECTION, IS THIS A MATTER FOR THE GODS?

Thasper obsessively wrote all these sayings down. He was obsessed again, he admitted, but this time it was in a new way. He
was thinking, thinking. At first he thought simply of clever questions to ask the Sage. He strained to find questions no one had
asked before. But in the process his mind seemed to loosen, and
shortly he was thinking of how the Sage might answer his questions. He considered order and rules and Heaven, and it came to
him that there was a reason behind all the brilliant questions the
Sage asked. He felt light-headed with thinking.

The reason behind the Sage's questions came to him the
morning he was shaving for the first time. He thought, The
gods need human beings in order to be gods! Blinded with this
revelation, Thasper stared into the mirror at his own face half
covered with white foam. Without humans believing in them,
gods were nothing! The order of Heaven, the rules and codes of
earth, were all only there because of people! It was transcendent.
As Thasper stared, the letter from the Unknown came into his
mind. "Is this being face to face with myself?" he said. But he
was not sure. And he became sure that when that time came, he
would not have to wonder.

Then it came to him that the Unknown Chrestomanci was almost certainly the Sage himself. He was thrilled. The Sage was
taking a special mysterious interest in one teenage boy, Thasper
Altun. The vanishing letter exactly fitted the elusive Sage.

The Sage continued elusive. The next firm news of him was a
newspaper report of the Celestial Gallery's being struck by lightning. The roof of the building collapsed, said the report, "only
seconds after the young man known as the Sage of Dissolution
had delivered another of his anguished and self-doubting homi-
lies and left the building with his disciples."

"He's not self-doubting," Thasper said to himself. "He knows about the gods. If *I* know, then *he* certainly does."

He and his classmates went on a pilgrimage to the ruined gallery. It was a better building than Small Unction Hall. It seemed the Sage was going up in the world.

Then there was enormous excitement. One of the girls found a small advertisement in a paper. The Sage was to deliver another lecture, in the huge Kingdom of Splendor Hall. He had gone up in the world again. Thasper and his friends dressed in their best and went there in a body. But it seemed as if the time for the lecture had been printed wrong. The lecture was just over. People were streaming away from the hall, looking disappointed.

Thasper and his friends were still in the street when the hall blew up. They were lucky not to be hurt. The police said it was a bomb. Thasper and his friends helped drag injured people clear of the blazing hall. It was exciting, but it was not the Sage.

By now Thasper knew he would never be happy until he had found the Sage. He told himself that he had to know if the reason behind the Sage's questions was the one he thought. But it was more than that. Thasper was convinced that his fate was linked to the Sage's. He was certain the Sage *wanted* Thasper to find him.

But there was now a strong rumor in school and around town that the Sage had had enough of lectures and bomb attacks. He had retired to write a book. It was to be called *Questions of Dissolution.* Rumor also had it that the Sage was in lodgings somewhere near the Road of the Four Lions.

Thasper went to the Road of the Four Lions. There he was shameless. He knocked on doors and questioned passers-by. He was told several times to go and ask an invisible dragon, but he took no notice. He went on asking until someone told him that Mrs. Tunap at No. 403 might know. Thasper knocked at No. 403, with his heart thumping.

Mrs. Tunap was a rather prim lady in a green turban. "I'm afraid not, dear," she said. "I'm new here." But before Thasper's heart could sink too far, she added, "But the people before me had a lodger. A very quiet gentleman. He left just before I came."

"Did he leave an address?" Thasper asked, holding his breath.

Mrs. Tunap consulted an old envelope pinned to the wall in her hall. "It says here, 'Lodger gone to Golden Heart Square,' dear."

But in Golden Heart Square, a young gentleman who might have been the Sage had only looked at a room and gone. After that Thasper had to go home. The Altuns were not used to teenagers, and they worried about Thasper suddenly wanting to be out every evening.

Oddly enough, No. 403 Road of the Four Lions burned down that night.

Thasper saw clearly that assassins were after the Sage as well as he was. He became more obsessed with finding him than ever. He knew he could rescue the Sage if he caught him before the assassins did. He did not blame the Sage for moving about all the time.

Move about the Sage certainly did. Rumor had him next in Partridge Pleasance Street. When Thasper tracked him there, he found the Sage had moved to Fauntel Square. From Fauntel Square, the Sage seemed to move to Strong Wind Boulevard, and then to a poorer house in Station Street. There were many places after that. By this time Thasper had developed a nose, a sixth sense, for where the Sage might be. A word, a mere hint about a quiet lodger, and Thasper was off, knocking on doors, questioning people, being told to ask an invisible dragon, and bewildering his parents by the way he kept rushing off every evening. But no matter how quickly Thasper acted on the latest hint, the Sage had always just left. And Thasper, in most cases, was only just ahead of the assassins. Houses caught fire or blew up, sometimes when he was still in the same street.

At last he was down to a very poor hint, which might or might not lead to New Unicorn Street. Thasper went there, wishing he did not have to spend all day at school. The Sage could move about as he pleased, and Thasper was tied down all day. No wonder he kept missing him. But he had high hopes of New Unicorn Street. It was the poor kind of place that the Sage had been favoring lately.

Alas for his hopes. The fat woman who opened the door laughed rudely in Thasper's face. "Don't bother me, son! Go and ask an invisible dragon!" And she slammed the door again.

Thasper stood in the street, keenly humiliated. And not even a hint of where to look next. Awful suspicions rose in his mind: he was making a fool of himself; he had set himself a wild-goose chase; the Sage did not exist. In order not to think of these things, he gave way to anger. "All right!" he shouted at the shut door. "I *will* ask an invisible dragon! So there!" And carried by his anger, he ran down to the river and out across the nearest bridge.

He stopped in the middle of the bridge, leaning on the parapet, and knew he was making an utter fool of himself. There were no such things as invisible dragons. He was sure of that. But he was still in the grip of his obsession, and this was something he had set himself to do now. Even so, if there had been anyone about near the bridge, Thasper would have gone away. But it was deserted. Feeling an utter fool, he made the prayer sign to Ock, Ruler of Oceans—for Ock was the god in charge of all things to do with water—but he made the sign secretly, down under the parapet, so there was no chance of anyone's seeing. Then he said, almost in a whisper, "Is there an invisible dragon here? I've got something to ask you."

Drops of water whirled over him. Something wetly fanned his face. He heard the something whirring. He turned his face that way and saw three blots of wet in a line along the parapet, each about two feet apart and each the size of two of his hands spread out together. Odder still, water was dripping out of nowhere all along the parapet, for a distance about twice as long as Thasper was tall.

Thasper laughed uneasily. "I'm imagining a dragon," he said. "If there was a dragon, those splotches would be the places where its body rests. Water dragons have no feet. And the length of the wetness suggests I must be imagining it about eleven feet long."

"I am fourteen feet long," said a voice out of nowhere. It was rather too near Thasper's face for comfort and blew fog at him. He drew back. "Make haste, child-of-a-god," said the voice. "What did you want to ask me?"

"I-I-I—" stammered Thasper. It was not just that he was scared. This was a body blow. It messed up utterly his notions about gods needing men to believe in them. But he pulled himself together. His voice only cracked a little as he said, "I'm looking for the Sage of Dissolution. Do you know where he is?"

The dragon laughed. It was a peculiar noise, like one of those water warblers people make bird noises with. "I'm afraid I can't tell you precisely where the Sage is," the voice out of nowhere said. "You have to find him for yourself. Think about it, child-of-a-god. You must have noticed there's a pattern."

"Too right, there's a pattern!" Thasper said. "Everywhere he goes, I just miss him, and then the place catches fire!"

"That, too," said the dragon. "But there's a pattern to his lodgings, too. Look for it. That's all I can tell you, child-of-a-god. Any other questions?"

"No—for a wonder," Thasper said. "Thanks very much."

"You're welcome," said the invisible dragon. "People are always telling one another to ask us, and hardly anyone does. I'll see you again." Watery air whirled in Thasper's face. He leaned over the parapet and saw one prolonged clean splash in the river, and silver bubbles coming up. Then nothing. He was surprised to find his legs were shaking.

He steadied his knees and tramped home. He went to his room, and before he did anything else, he acted on a superstitious impulse he had not thought he had in him and took down the household god Alina insisted he keep in a niche over his bed. He put it carefully outside in the passage. Then he got out a map of the town and some red stickers and plotted out all the places where he had just missed the Sage. The result had him dancing with excitement. The dragon was right. There was a pattern. The Sage had started in good lodgings at the better end of town. Then he had gradually moved to poorer places, but he had moved in a curve, down to the station and back toward the better part again. Now, the Altuns' house was just on the edge of the poorer part. The Sage was *coming this way*! New Unicorn Street had not been so far away. The next place should be nearer still. Thasper had only to look for a house on fire.

It was getting dark by then. Thasper threw his curtains back and leaned out of his window to look at the poorer streets. And there it was! There was a red-and-orange flicker to the left—in Harvest Moon Street, by the look of it. Thasper laughed aloud. He was actually grateful to the assassins!

He raced downstairs and out of the house. The anxious questions of parents and the yells of brothers and sisters followed him, but he slammed the door on them. Two minutes' running brought him to the scene of the fire. The street was a mad flicker of dark figures. People were piling furniture in the road. Some more people were helping a dazed woman in a crooked brown turban into a singed armchair.

"Didn't you have a lodger as well?" someone asked her anxiously.

The woman kept trying to straighten her turban. It was all she could really think of. "He didn't stay," she said. "I think he may be down at the Half Moon now."

Thasper waited for no more. He went pelting down the street.

The Half Moon was an inn on the corner of the same road. Most of the people who usually drank there must have been up the street, helping rescue furniture, but there was a dim light inside, enough to show a white notice in the window. ROOMS, it said.

Thasper burst inside. The barman was on a stool by the window, craning to watch the house burn. He did not look at Thasper. "Where's your lodger?" gasped Thasper. "I've got a message. Urgent."

The barman did not turn around. "Upstairs, first on the left," he said. "The roof's caught. They'll have to act quick to save the house on either side."

Thasper heard him say this as he bounded upstairs. He turned left. He gave the briefest of knocks on the door there, flung it open, and rushed in.

The room was empty. The light was on, and it showed a stark bed, a stained table with an empty mug and some sheets of paper on it, and a fireplace with a mirror over it. Beside the fireplace, another door was just swinging shut. Obviously somebody had just that moment gone through it. Thasper bounded toward that door. But he was checked, for just a second, by seeing himself in the mirror over the fireplace. He had not meant to pause. But some trick of the mirror, which was old and brown and speckled, made his reflection look for a moment a great deal older. He looked easily over twenty. He looked—

He remembered the Letter from the Unknown. This was the time. He knew it was. He was about to meet the Sage. He had only to call him. Thasper went toward the still gently swinging door. He hesitated. The letter had said call at once. Knowing the Sage was just beyond the door, Thasper pushed it open a fraction and held it so with his fingers. He was full of doubts. He thought, Do I really believe the gods need people? Am I so sure? What shall I say to the Sage after all? He let the door slip shut again.

"Chrestomanci," he said miserably.

There was a *whoosh* of displaced air behind him. It buffeted Thasper half around. He stared. A tall man was standing by the stark bed. He was a most extraordinary figure in a long black robe, with what seemed to be yellow comets embroidered on it. The inside of the robe, swirling in the air, showed yellow, with black comets on it. The tall man had a very smooth dark head, very bright dark eyes, and, on his feet, what seemed to be red bedroom slippers.

"Thank goodness," said this outlandish person. "For a moment I was afraid you would go through that door."

The voice brought memory back to Thasper. "You brought me home through a picture when I was little," he said. "Are you Chrestomanci?"

"Yes," said the tall, outlandish man. "And you are Thasper. And now we must both leave before this building catches fire."

He took hold of Thasper's arm and towed him to the door which led to the stairs. As soon as he pushed the door open, thick smoke rolled in, filled with harsh crackling. It was clear that the inn was on fire already. Chrestomanci clapped the door shut again. The smoke set both of them coughing, Chrestomanci so violently that Thasper was afraid he would choke. He pulled both of them back into the middle of the room. By now smoke was twining up between the bare boards of the floor, causing Chrestomanci to cough again.

"This would happen just as I had gone to bed with flu," he said, when he could speak. "Such is life. These orderly gods of yours leave us no choice." He crossed the smoking floor and pushed open the door by the fireplace.

It opened onto blank space. Thasper gave a yelp of horror.

"Precisely," coughed Chrestomanci. "You were intended to crash to your death."

"Can't we jump to the ground?" Thasper suggested.

Chrestomanci shook his smooth head. "Not after they've done this to it. No. We'll have to carry the fight to them and go and visit the gods instead. Will you be kind enough to lend me your turban before we go?" Thasper stared at this odd request. "I would like to use it as a belt," Chrestomanci croaked. "The way to Heaven may be a little cold, and I only have pajamas under my dressing gown."

The striped undergarments Chrestomanci was wearing did look a little thin. Thasper slowly unwound his turban. To go before gods bareheaded was probably no worse than going in nightclothes, he supposed. Besides, he did not believe there were any gods. He handed the turban over. Chrestomanci tied the length of pale blue cloth around his black-and-yellow gown and seemed to feel more comfortable. "Now hang on to me," he said, "and you'll be all right." He took Thasper's arm again and walked up into the sky, dragging Thasper with him.

For a while Thasper was too stunned to speak. He could only marvel at the way they were treading up the sky as if there were invisible stairs in it. Chrestomanci was doing it in the most matter-of-fact way, coughing from time to time and shivering a little, but keeping very tight hold of Thasper nevertheless. In no time the town was a clutter of prettily lit dolls' houses below, with two red blots where two of them were burning. The stars were unwinding about them, above and below, as if they had already climbed above some of them.

"It's a long climb to Heaven," Chrestomanci observed. "Is there anything you'd like to know on the way?"

"Yes," said Thasper. "Did you say the gods are trying to kill me?"

"They are trying to eliminate the Sage of Dissolution," said Chrestomanci, "which they may not realize is the same thing. You see, you are the Sage."

"But I'm not!" Thasper insisted. "The Sage is a lot older than me, and he asks questions I never even thought of until I heard of him."

"Ah yes," said Chrestomanci. "I'm afraid there is an awful circularity to this. It's the fault of whoever tried to put you away as a small child. As far as I can work out, you stayed three years old for seven years—until you were making such a disturbance in our world that we had to find you and let you out. But in this world of Theare, highly organized and fixed as it is, the prophecy stated that you would begin preaching Dissolution at the age of twenty-three, or at least in this very year. Therefore the preaching had to begin this year. You did not need to appear. Did you ever speak to anyone who had actually heard the Sage preach?"

"No," said Thasper. "Come to think of it."

"Nobody did," said Chrestomanci. "You started in a small way, anyway. First you wrote a book, which no one paid much heed to—"

"No, that's wrong," objected Thasper. "He—I—er, the Sage was writing a book *after* the preaching."

"But don't you see," said Chrestomanci, "because you were back in Theare by then, the facts had to try to catch you up. They did this by running backward, until it was possible for you to arrive where you were supposed to be. Which was in that room in the inn there, at the start of your career. I suppose you are just old enough to start by now. And I suspect our celestial friends up here tumbled to this belatedly and tried to finish you off. It wouldn't have done them any good, as I shall shortly tell them." He began coughing again. They had climbed to where it was bitterly cold.

By this time the world was a dark arch below them. Thasper could see the blush of the sun, beginning to show underneath the world. They climbed on. The light grew. The sun appeared, a huge brightness in the distance underneath. A dim memory came again to Thasper. He struggled to believe that none of this was true, and he did not succeed.

"How do you know all this?" he asked bluntly.

"Have you heard of a god called Ock?" Chrestomanci coughed. "He came to talk to me when you should have been the age you are now. He was worried—" He coughed again. "I shall have to save the rest of my breath for Heaven."

They climbed on, and the stars swam around them, until the stuff they were climbing changed and became solider. Soon they were climbing a dark ramp, which flushed pearly as they went upward. Here Chrestomanci let go of Thasper's arm and blew his nose on a gold-edged handkerchief with an air of relief. The pearl of the ramp grew to silver and the silver to dazzling white. At length they were walking on level whiteness, through hall after hall.

The gods were gathered to meet them. None of them looked cordial.

"I fear we are not properly dressed," Chrestomanci murmured.

Thasper looked at the gods, and then at Chrestomanci, and squirmed with embarrassment. Fanciful and queer as Chrestomanci's garb was, it was still most obviously nightwear. The things on his feet were fur bedroom slippers. And there, looking like a piece of blue string around Chrestomanci's waist, was the turban Thasper should have been wearing. The gods were magnificent, in golden trousers and jeweled turbans, and got more so as they approached the greater gods. Thasper's eye was caught by a god in shining cloth of gold, who surprised him by beaming a friendly, almost anxious look at him. Opposite him was a huge, liquid-looking figure draped in pearls and diamonds. This god swiftly, but quite definitely, winked. Thasper was too awed to react, but Chrestomanci calmly winked back.

At the end of the halls, upon a massive throne, towered the mighty figure of Great Zond, clothed in white and purple, with a crown on his head. Chrestomanci looked up at Zond and thoughtfully blew his nose. It was hardly respectful.

"For what reason do two mortals trespass in our halls?" Zond thundered coldly.

Chrestomanci sneezed. "Because of your own folly," he said. "You gods of Theare have had everything so well worked out for so long that you can't see beyond your own routine."

"I shall blast you for that," Zond announced.

"Not if any of you wish to survive," Chrestomanci said.

There was a long murmur of protest from the other gods. They wished to survive. They were trying to work out what Chrestomanci meant. Zond saw it as a threat to his authority and thought he had better be cautious. "Proceed," he said.

"One of your most efficient features," Chrestomanci said, "is that your prophecies always come true. So why, when a prophecy is unpleasant to you, do you think you can alter it? That, my good gods, is rank folly. Besides, no one can halt his own Dissolution, least of all you gods of Theare. But you forgot. You forgot you had deprived both yourselves and mankind of any kind of free will, by organizing yourselves so precisely. You pushed Thasper, the Sage of Dissolution, into my world, forgetting that there is still chance in my world. By chance, Thasper was discovered after only seven years. Lucky for Theare that he was. I shudder to think what might have happened if Thasper had remained three years old for all his allotted lifetime."

"That was my fault!" cried Imperion. "I take the blame." He

turned to Thasper. "Forgive me," he said. "You are my own son."

Was this, Thasper wondered, what Alina meant by the gods blessing her womb? He had not thought it was more than a figure of speech. He looked at Imperion, blinking a little in the god's dazzle. He was not wholly impressed. A fine god, and an honest one, but Thasper could see he had a limited outlook. "Of course I forgive you," he said politely.

"It is also lucky," Chrestomanci said, "that none of you succeeded in killing the Sage. Thasper is a god's son. That means there can only ever be one of him, and because of your prophecy, he has to be alive to preach Dissolution. You could have destroyed Theare. As it is, you have caused it to blur into a mass of cracks. Theare is too well organized to divide into two alternative worlds, as my world would. Instead, events have had to happen which could not have happened. Theare has cracked and warped, and you have all but brought about your own Dissolution."

"What can we do?" Zond said, aghast.

"There's only one thing you can do," Chrestomanci told him. "Let Thasper be. Let him preach Dissolution and stop trying to blow him up. That will bring about free will and a free future. Then either Theare will heal, or it will split, cleanly and painlessly, into two healthy new worlds."

"So we bring about our own downfall?" Zond asked mournfully.

"It was always inevitable," said Chrestomanci.

Zond sighed. "Very well. Thasper, son of Imperion, I reluctantly give you my blessing to go forth and preach Dissolution. Go in peace."

Thasper bowed. Then he stood there silent a long time. He did not notice Imperion and Ock both trying to attract his attention. The newspaper report had talked of the Sage as full of anguish and self-doubt. Now he knew why. He looked at Chrestomanci, who was blowing his nose again. "How can I preach Dissolution?" he said. "How can I not believe in the gods when I have seen them for myself?"

"That's a question you certainly should be asking," Chrestomanci croaked. "Go down to Theare and ask it." Thasper nodded and turned to go. Chrestomanci leaned toward him and said, from behind his handkerchief, "Ask yourself this, too: can the gods catch flu? I think I may have given it to all of them. Find out and let me know, there's a good chap."

THE MASTER

This is the trouble with being a newly qualified vet. The call came at 5:50 A.M. I thought it was a man's voice, though it was high for a man, and I didn't quite catch the name—Harry Sanovit? Harrison Ovett? Anyway, he said it was urgent.

Accordingly, I found myself on the edge of a plain, facing a dark fir forest. It was about midmorning. The fir trees stood dark and evenly spaced, exhaling their crackling gummy scent, with vistas of trodden-looking pine needles beneath them. A wolfwood, I thought. I was sure that thought was right. The spacing of the trees was so regular that it suggested an artificial pinewood in the zoo, and there was a kind of humming, far down at the edges of the senses, as if machinery was at work sustaining a man-made environment here. The division between trees and plain was so sharp that I had some doubts that I would be able to enter the wood.

But I stepped inside with no difficulty. Under the trees it was cooler, more strongly scented, and full of an odd kind of depression, which made me sure that there was some sort of danger here. I walked on the carpet of needles cautiously, relaxed but intensely afraid. There seemed to be some kind of path winding between the straight boles, and I followed it into the heart of the wood. After a few turns, flies buzzed around something just off the path. *Danger!* pricked out all over my skin like sweat, but I went and looked all the same.

It was a young woman about my own age. From the flies and the freshness, I would have said she had been killed only hours ago. Her throat had been torn out. The expression on her half-averted face was of sheer terror. She had glorious red hair and was wearing what looked, improbably, to be evening dress.

I backed away, swallowing. As I backed, something came up beside me. I whirled around with a croak of terror.

"No need to fear," he said. "I am only the fool."

He was very tall and thin and ungainly. His feet were in big, laced boots, jigging a silent, ingratiating dance on the pine needles, and the rest of his clothes were a dull brown and close-fitting. His huge hands came out to me placatingly. "I am Egbert," he said. "You may call me Eggs. You will take no harm if you stay with me." His eyes slid off mine apologetically, round and blue-gray. He grinned all over his small, inane face. Under his close crop of straw-fair hair, his face was indeed that of a near idiot. He did not seem to notice the woman's corpse at all, even though he seemed to know I was full of horror.

"What's going on here?" I asked him helplessly. "I'm a vet, not a—not a—mortician. What animal needs me?"

He smiled seraphically at nothing over my left shoulder. "I am only Eggs, Lady. I don't not know nothing. What you need to do is call the Master. Then you will know."

"So where is the Master?" I said.

He looked baffled by this question. "Hereabouts," he suggested. He gave another beguiling smile, over my right shoulder this time, panting slightly. "He will come if you call him right. Will I show you the house, Lady? There are rare sights there."

"Yes, if you like," I said. Anything to get away from whatever had killed that girl. Besides, I trusted him somehow. When he had said I would take no harm if I was with him, it had been said in a way I believed.

He turned and cavorted up the path ahead of me, skipping soundlessly on his great feet, waving great, gangling arms, clumsily tripping over a tree root and, even more clumsily, just saving himself. He held his head on one side and hummed as he went, happy and harmless. That is to say, harmless to me so far. Though he walked like a great, hopping puppet, those huge hands were certainly strong enough to rip a throat out.

"Who killed that girl?" I asked him. "Was it the Master?"

His head snapped around, swayingly, and he stared at me, appalled, balancing on the path as though it were a tightrope. "Oh, no, Lady. The Master wouldn't not do that!" He turned sadly, almost tearfully, away.

"I'm sorry," I said.

His head bent, acknowledging that he had heard, but he continued to walk the tightrope of the path without answering, and I followed. As I did, I was aware that there was something moving among the trees to either side of us. Something softly kept pace with us there, and, I was sure, something also followed along the path behind. I did not try to see what it was. I was quite as much angry with myself as I was scared. I had let my shock at seeing that corpse get the better of my judgment. I saw I must wait to find out how the redheaded girl had got herself killed. Caution! I said to myself. Caution! This path was a tightrope indeed.

"Has the Master got a name?" I asked.

That puzzled Eggs. He stood balancing on the path to think. After a moment he nodded doubtfully, shot me a shy smile over his shoulder, and walked on. No attempt to ask my name, I noticed. As if I was the only other person there and "Lady" should be enough. Which meant that the presences among the trees and behind on the path were possibly not human.

Around the next bend I found myself facing the veranda of a chaletlike building. It looked a little as if it were made of wood, but it was no substance that I knew. Eggs tripped on the step and floundered toward the door at the back of the veranda. Before I could make more than a move to help him, he had saved himself and his great hands were groping with an incomprehensible lock on the door. The humming was more evident here. I had been hoping that what I had heard at the edge of the wood had been the flies on the corpse. It was not. Though the sound was still not much more than a vibration at the edge of the mind, I knew I had been right in my first idea. Something artificial was being maintained here, and whatever was maintaining it seemed to be under this house.

In this house, I thought, as Eggs got the door open and floundered inside ahead of me. The room we entered was full of—well, devices. The nearest thing was a great cauldron, softly bubbling for no reason I could see, and giving out a gauzy violet light. The other things were arranged in ranks beyond, bewilderingly. In one place something grotesque stormed green inside a design painted on the floor; here a copper bowl smoked; there a single candle sat like something holy on a white stone; a knife suspended in air dripped gently into a jar of rainbow glass. Much of it was glass, twinkling, gleaming, chiming, under the light from the low ceiling that seemed to come from nowhere. There were no windows.

"Good heavens!" I said, disguising my dismay as amazement. "What are all these?"

Eggs grinned. "I know some. Pretty, aren't they?" He roved, surging about, touching the edge of a pattern here, passing his huge hand through a flame or a column of smoke there, causing a shower of fleeting white stars, solemn gong notes, and a rich smell of incense. "Pretty, aren't they?" he kept repeating, and, "*Very* pretty!" as an entire fluted glass structure began to ripple and change shape at the end of the room. As it changed, the humming, which was everywhere in the room, changed, too. It became a purring chime, and I felt an indescribable pulling feeling from the roots of my hair and under my skin, almost as if the glass thing were trying to change me as it changed itself.

"I should come away from that if I were you," I said as firmly and calmly as I could manage.

Eggs turned and came floundering toward me, grinning eagerly. To my relief, the sound from the glass modulated to a new kind of humming. But my relief vanished when Eggs said, "Petra knew all, before Annie tore her throat out. Do you know as much as Petra? You are clever, Lady, as well as beautiful." His eyes slid across me, respectfully. Then he turned and hung, lurching, over the cauldron with the gauzy violet light. "Petra took pretty dresses from here," he said. "Would you like for me to get you a pretty dress?"

"Not at the moment, thank you," I said, trying to sound kind. As I said, Eggs was not necessarily harmless. "Show me the rest of the house," I said, to distract him.

He fell over his feet to oblige. "Come. See here." He led me to the side of the devices, where there was a clear passage and some doors. At the back of the room was another door, which slid open by itself as we came near. Eggs giggled proudly at that, as if it were his doing. Beyond was evidently a living room. The floor here was soft, carpetlike, and blue. Darker blue blocks hung about, mysteriously half a meter or so in the air. Four of them were a meter or so square. The fifth was two meters each way. They had the look of a suite of chairs and a sofa to me. A squiggly mural thing occupied one wall, and the entire end wall was window, which seemed to lead to another veranda, beyond which I could see a garden of some kind. "The room is pretty, isn't it?" Eggs asked anxiously. "I like the room."

I assured him I liked the room. This relieved him. He stumbled around a floating blue block, which was barely disturbed by his falling against it, and pressed a plate in the wall beyond. The long glass of the window slid back, leaving the room open to the veranda. He turned to me, beaming.

"Clever," I said, and made another cautious attempt to find out more. "Did Petra show you how to open that, or was it the Master?"

He was puzzled again. "I don't not know," he said, worried about it.

I gave up and suggested we go into the garden. He was pleased. We went over the veranda and down steps into a rose garden. It was an oblong shape, carved out from among the fir trees, about fifteen meters from the house to the bushy hedge at the far end. And it was as strange as everything else. The square of sky overhead was subtly the wrong color, as if you were seeing it through sunglasses. It made the color of the roses rich and too dark. I walked through with a certainty that it was being maintained—or created—by one of the devices in that windowless room.

The roses were all standards, each planted in a little circular bed. The head of each was about level with my head. No petals fell on the gravel-seeming paths. I kept exclaiming, because these were the most perfect roses I ever saw, whether full bloom, bud, or overblown. When I saw an orange rose—the color I love most—I put my hand up cautiously to make sure that it was real. It was. While my fingers lingered on it, I happened to glance at Eggs, towering over me. It was just a flick of the eyes, which I don't think he saw. He was standing there, smiling as always, staring at me intently. There was, I swear, another shape to his face, and it was not the shape of an idiot. But it was not the shape of a normal man either. It was an intent, *hunting* face.

Next moment he was surging inanely forward. "I will pick you a rose, Lady." He reached out and stumbled as he reached. His hand caught a thorn in a tumble of petals. He snatched it back with a yelp. "Oh!" he said. "It hurts!" He lifted his hand and stared at it. Blood was running down the length of his little finger.

"Suck it," I said. "Is the thorn still in it?"

"I don't know," Eggs said helplessly. Several drops of blood had fallen among the fallen petals before he took my advice and sucked the cut, noisily. As he did so, his other hand came forward to bar my way. "Stay by me, Lady," he said warningly.

I had already stopped dead. Whether they had been there all

along or had been summoned, materialized, by the scent of blood, I still do not know, but they were there now, against the hedge at the end of the garden, all staring at me. Three Alsatian dogs, I told myself foolishly, and knew it was nonsense as I thought it. Three of them. Three wolves. Each of them must have been, in bulk, if not in height, at least as big as I was.

They were dark in the curious darkness of that garden. Their eyes were the easiest to see, light wolf-green. All of them staring at me, staring earnestly, hungrily. The smaller two were crouched in front. One of those was brindled and larger and rangier than his browner companion. And these two were only small by comparison with the great black she-wolf standing behind with slaver running from her open jaws. She was poised either to pounce or to run away. I have never seen anything more feral than that black she-wolf. But they were all feral, stiff-legged, terrified, half in mind to tear my throat out, and yet they were held there for some reason, simply staring. All three were soundlessly snarling, even before I spoke.

My horror—caught from the wolves to some extent—was beyond thought and out into a dreamlike state, where I simply knew that Eggs was right when he said I would be safe with him, and so I said what the dream seemed to require. "Eggs," I said, "tell me their names."

Eggs was quite unperturbed. His hand left his mouth and pointed at the brindled wolf in front. "That one is Hugh, Lady. Theo is the one beside him. She standing at the back is Annie."

So now I knew what had torn redheaded Petra's throat out. And what kind of woman was she, I wondered, who must have had Eggs as servant and a roomful of strange devices, and on top of this gave three wild beasts these silly names? My main thought was that I did not want my throat torn out, too. And I had been called here as a vet after all. It took quite an effort to look those three creatures over professionally, but I did so. Ribs showed under the curly brownish coat of Theo. Hugh's haunches stuck out like knives. As for Annie standing behind, her belly clung upward almost to her backbone. "When did they last eat?" I said.

Eggs smiled at me. "There is food in the forest for them, Lady."

I stared at him, but he seemed to have no idea what he was saying. It was to the wolves' credit that they did not seem to regard dead Petra as food, but from the look of them it would not be long before they did so. "Eggs," I said, "these three are starving. You and I must go back into the house and find food for them."

Eggs seemed much struck by this idea. "Clever," he said. "I am only the fool, Lady." And as I turned, gently, not to alarm the wolves, he stretched out his hands placatingly—at least it looked placating, but it was quite near to an attempt to take hold of me, a sketch of it, as it were. That alarmed me, but I dared not show it here. The wolves' ears pricked a little as we moved off up the garden, but they did not move, to my great relief.

Back through the house Eggs led me in his lurching, puppet's gait, around the edges of the room with the devices, where the humming filled the air and still seemed to drag at me in a way I did not care for at all, to another brightly lit, windowless room on the other side. It was a kitchen place, furnished in what seemed to be glass. Here Eggs cannoned into a glass table and stopped short, looking at me expectantly. I gazed around at glass-fronted apparatus, some of it full of crockery, some of it clearly food stores, with food heaped behind the glass, and some of it quite mysterious to me. I made for the glass cupboard full of various joints of meat. I could see they were fresh, although the thing was clearly not a refrigerator. "How do you open this?" I asked.

Eggs looked down at his great hands, planted in encircling vapor on top of the glass table. "I don't not know, Lady."

I could have shaken him. Instead, I clawed at the edges of the cupboard. Nothing happened. There it was, warmish, piled with a good fifty kilograms of meat, while three starving wolves prowled outside, and nothing I could do seemed to have any effect on the smooth edge of the glass front. At length I pried my fingernails under the top edge and pulled, thinking it moved slightly.

Eggs's huge hand knocked against mine, nudging me awkwardly away. "No, no, Lady. That way you'll get hurt. It is under stass-spell, see." For a moment he fumbled doubtfully at the top rim of the glass door, but, when I made a movement to come back and help, his hands suddenly moved, smoothly and surely. The thing clicked. The glass slid open downward, and the smell of meat rolled out into the kitchen.

So you *do* know how to do it! I thought. And I *knew* you did! There was some hint he had given me, I knew, as I reached for the nearest joint, which I could not quite see now.

"No, *no,* Lady!" This time Eggs pushed me aside hard. He was really distressed. "Never put hand into stass-spell. It will die on you. You do this." He took up a long, shiny pair of tongs, which I had not noticed because they were nested into the top of the cupboard, and grasped the nearest joint with them. "This, Lady?"

"And two more," I said. "And when did you last eat, Eggs?" He shrugged and looked at me, baffled. "Then get out those two steaks, too," I said. Eggs seemed quite puzzled, but he fetched out the meat. "Now we must find water for them as well," I said.

"But there is juice here in this corner!" Eggs objected. "See." He went to one of the mysterious fixtures and shortly came back with a sort of cardboard cup swaying in one hand, which he handed me to taste, staring eagerly while I did. "Good?" he asked.

It was some form of alcohol. "Very good," I said, "but not for wolves." It took me half an hour of patient work to persuade Eggs to fetch out a large lightweight bowl and then to manipulate a queer faucet to fill it with water. He could not see the point of it at all. I was precious near to hitting him before long. I was quite glad when he stayed behind in the kitchen to shut the cabinets and finish his cup of "juice."

The wolves had advanced down the garden. I could see their pricked ears and their eyes above the veranda boards, but they did not move when I stepped out onto the veranda. I had to make myself move with a calmness and slowness I was far from feeling. Deliberately I dropped each joint, one by one, with a sticky thump onto the strange surface. From the size and the coarse grain of the meat, it seemed to be venison—at least I hoped it was. Then I carefully lowered the bowl to stand at the far end of the veranda, looking all the time through my hair at the wolves. They did not move, but the open jaws of the big wolf, Annie, were dripping.

The bowl down, I backed away into the living room, where I just had to sit down on the nearest blue block. My knees gave.

They did not move for long seconds. Then all three disappeared below the veranda, and I thought they must have slunk away. But the two smaller ones reappeared, suddenly, silently, as if they had materialized, at the end of the veranda beside the bowl. Tails trailing, shaking all over, they crept toward it. Both stuck their muzzles in and drank avidly. I could hear their frantic lapping. And when they raised their heads, which they both did shortly, neatly and disdainfully, I realized that one of the joints of meat had gone. The great wolf, Annie, had been and gone.

Her speed must have reassured Theo and Hugh. Both sniffed the air, then fumed and trotted toward the remaining joints.

Each nosed a joint. Each picked it up neatly in his jaws. Theo seemed about to jump down into the garden with his. But Hugh, to my astonishment, came straight toward the open window, evidently intending to eat on the carpet as dogs do.

He never got a chance. Theo dropped his joint and sprang at him with a snarl. There was the heavy squeak of clawed paws. Hugh sprang around, hackles rising the length of his lean, sloping back, and snarled back without dropping his portion. It was, he seemed to be saying, his own business where he went to eat. Theo, crouching, advancing on him with lowered head and white teeth showing, was clearly denying him this right. I braced myself for the fight. But at that moment Annie reappeared, silent as ever, head and great forepaws on the edge of the veranda, and stood there, poised. Theo and Hugh vanished like smoke, running long and low to either side. Both took their food with them, to my relief. Annie dropped out of sight again. Presently there were faint, very faint, sounds of eating from below.

I went back to the glassy kitchen, where I spent the next few hours getting Eggs to eat, too. He did not seem to regard anything in the kitchen as edible. It took me a good hour to persuade him to open a vegetable cabinet and quite as long to persuade him to show me how to cook the food. If I became insistent, he said, "I don't not know, Lady," lost interest, and shuffled off to the windowless room to play with the pretty lights. That alarmed me. Every time I fetched him back, the humming chime from the glass apparatus seemed to drag at me more intensely. I tried pleading. "Eggs, I'm going to cut these yams, but I can't find a knife somehow." That worked better. Eggs would come over obligingly and find me a thing like a prong and then wander off to his "juice" again. There were times when I thought we were going to have to eat everything raw.

But it got done in the end. Eggs showed me how to ignite a

terrifying heat source that was totally invisible, and I fried the food on it in a glass skillet. Most of the vegetables were quite strange to me, but at least the steak was recognizable. We were just sitting down on glass stools to eat it at the glass table when a door I had not realized was there slid aside beside me. The garden was beyond. The long snout of Hugh poked through the gap. The pale eyes met mine, and the wet nose quivered wistfully.

"What do you want?" I said, and I knew I had jerked with fear. It was obvious what Hugh wanted. The garden must have filled with the smell of cooking. But I had not realized that the wolves could get into the kitchen when they pleased. Trying to seem calm, I tossed Hugh some fat I'd trimmed off the steaks. He caught it neatly and, to my intense relief, backed out of the door, which closed behind him.

I was almost too shaken to eat after that, but Eggs ate his share with obvious pleasure, though he kept glancing at me as if he was afraid I would think he was making a pig of himself. It was both touching and irritating. But the food—and the "juice"—did him good. His face became pinker, and he did not jig so much. I began to risk a few cautious questions. "Eggs, did Petra live in this house or just work here?"

He looked baffled. "I don't not know."

"But she used the wolves to help her in her work, didn't she?" It seemed clear to me that they *must* have been laboratory animals in some way.

Eggs shifted on his stool. "I don't not know," he said unhappily.

"And did the Master help in the work, too?" I persisted.

But this was too much for Eggs. He sprang up in agitation, and before I could stop him, he swept everything off the table into a large receptacle near the door. "I can't say!" I heard him say above the crash of breaking crockery.

After that he would listen to nothing I said. His one idea was that we must go to the living room. "To sit elegantly, Lady," he explained. "And I will bring the sweet foods and the juice to enjoy ourselves with there."

There seemed no stopping him. He surged out of the kitchen with an armload of peculiar receptacles and a round jug of "juice" balanced between those and his chin, weaving this way and that among the devices in the windowless room. These flared and flickered and the unsupported knife danced in the air as I pursued him. I felt as much as saw the fluted glass structure changing shape again. The sound of it dragged at the very roots of me.

"Eggs," I said desperately. "How do I call the Master? Please."

"I can't say," he said, reeling on into the living room.

Some enlightenment came to me. Eggs meant exactly what he said. I had noticed that when he said "I don't *not* know," this did not mean that he did not know; it usually seemed to be something he could not explain. Now I saw that when he said "I can't say," he meant that he was, for some reason, unable to tell me about the Master. So, I thought, struggling on against the drag of the chiming apparatus, this means I must use a little cunning to get him to tell me.

In the living room Eggs was laying out dishes of sweets and little balls of cheese near the center of the large blue sofa-like block. I sat down—at one end of it. Eggs promptly came and sat beside me, grinning and breathing "juice" fumes. I got up and moved to the other end of the sofa. Eggs took the hint. He stayed where he was, sighing, and poured himself another papery cup of his "juice."

"Eggs," I began. Then I noticed that the wolf Hugh was crouched on the veranda facing into the room, with his brindled nose on his paws and his sharp haunches outlined against the sunset roses. Beyond him were the backs of the two others, apparently asleep. Well, wolves always leave at least one of their pack on guard when they sleep. I told myself that Hugh had drawn sentry duty and went back to thinking how I could induce Eggs to tell me how to get hold of this Master. By this time I felt I would go mad unless someone explained this situation to me.

"Eggs"—I began again—"when I ask you how I fetch the Master, you tell me you can't say, isn't that right?" He nodded eagerly, obligingly, and offered me a sweet. I took it. I was doing well so far. "That means that something's stopping you telling me, doesn't it?" That lost him. His eyes slid from mine. I looked where his eyes went and found that Hugh had been moving, in the unnoticed silent way a wild creature can. He was now crouched right inside the room. The light feral eyes were fixed on me. Help! I thought. But I had to go on with what I was saying before Eggs's crazed mind lost it. "So I'm going to take it that when you say, 'I can't say,' you mean 'Yes,' Eggs. It's going to be like a game."

Eggs's face lit up. "I like games, Lady!"

"Good," I said. "The game is called Calling-the-Master. Now I know you can't tell me direct how to call him, but the rule is that you're allowed to give me hints."

That was a mistake. "And what is the hint, Lady?" Eggs asked, in the greatest delight. "Tell me and I will give it."

"Oh—I—er—" I said. And I felt something cold gently touch my hand. I looked down to find Hugh standing by my knees. Beyond him Theo was standing up, bristling. "What do you want now?" I said to Hugh. His eyes slid across the plates of sweets, and he sighed, like a dog. "Not sweets," I said firmly. Hugh understood. He laid his long head on my knee, yearningly.

This produced a snarl from Theo out on the veranda. It sounded like pure jealousy.

"You can come in, too, if you want, Theo," I said hastily.

Theo gave no sign of understanding, but when I next looked, he was half across the threshold. He was crouched, not lying. His hackles were up, and his eyes glared at Hugh. Hugh's eyes moved to see where he was, but he did not raise his chin from my knee.

All this so unnerved me that I tried to explain what a hint was by telling Eggs a story. I should have known better. "In this story," I said, absently stroking Hugh's head as if he were my dog. Theo instantly rose to his feet with the lips of his muzzle drawn back and his ears up. I removed my hand—but quick! "In this story," I said. Theo lay down again, but now it was me he was glaring at. "A lady was left three boxes by her father, one box gold, one silver, and one lead. In one of the boxes there was a picture of her. Her father's orders were that the man who guessed which of the three boxes her picture was in could marry her—"

Eggs bounced up with a triumphant laugh. "I know! It was in the lead box! Lead protects. I can marry her!" He rolled about in delight. "Are you that lady?" he asked eagerly.

I suppressed a strong need to run about screaming. I was sure that if I did, either Theo or Annie would go for me. I was not sure about Hugh. He seemed to have been a house pet. "Right," I said. "It *was* in the lead box, Eggs. This *other* lady knew that, but the men who wanted to marry her had to guess. All of them guessed wrong, until one day a beautiful man came along whom this *other* lady wanted to marry. So what did she do?"

"Told him," said Eggs.

"No, she was forbidden to do that," I said. *God give me patience!* "Just like you. She had to give the man hints instead. Just like you. Before he came to choose the box, she got people to sing him a song and—remember, it was the *lead* box—every line in that song rhymed with 'lead.' A rhyme is a word that sounds the same," I added hurriedly, seeing bewilderment cloud Eggs's face. "You know—'said' and 'bled' and 'red' all rhyme with 'lead.'"

"Said, bled, red," Eggs repeated, quite lost.

"Dead, head," I said. Hugh's cold nose nudged my hand again. Wolves are not usually scavengers, unless in dire need, but I thought cheese would not hurt him. I passed him a round to keep him quiet.

Theo sprang up savagely and came half across the room. At the same instant, Eggs grasped what a rhyme was. "Fed, instead, bed, wed!" he shouted, rolling about with glee. I stared into Theo's gray-green glare and at his pleated lip showing the fangs beneath it and prayed to heaven. Very slowly and carefully, I rolled a piece of cheese off the sofa toward him. Theo swung away from it and stalked back to the window. "My hint is bed-spread, Lady!" Eggs shouted.

Hugh, meanwhile, calmly took his cheese as deftly and gently as any hunting dog and sprang up onto the sofa beside me, where he stood with his head down, chewing with small bites to make the cheese last. "Now you've done it, Hugh!" I said, look-ing nervously at Theo's raked-up back and at the sharp outline of Annie beyond him.

"Thread, head, watershed, bread!" bawled Eggs. I realized he was drunk. His face was flushed, and his eyes glittered. He had been putting back quantities of "juice" ever since he first showed me the kitchen. "Do I get to marry you now, Lady?" he asked soulfully.

Before I could think what to reply, Hugh moved across like lightning and bit Eggs on his nearest large folded knee. He jumped clear even quicker, as Eggs surged to his feet, and streaked off to join Theo on the veranda. I heard Theo snap at him.

Eggs took an uncertain step that way, then put his hand to his face. "What is this?" he said. "This room is chasing its tail." It was clear the "juice" had caught up with him.

"I think you're drunk," I said.

"Drink," said Eggs. "I must get a drink from the faucet. I am dying. It is worse than being remade." And he went blundering and crashing off into the windowless room.

I jumped up and went after him, sure that he would do untold damage bumping into cauldron or candle. But he wove his way through the medley of displays as only a drunk man can, avoiding each one by a miracle, and reached the kitchen when I was only halfway through the room. The hum of the crystal apparatus held me back. It dragged at my very skin. I had still only reached the cauldron when there was an appalling splintering crash from the kitchen, followed by a hoarse male scream.

I do not remember how I got to the kitchen. I only remember standing in the doorway, looking at Eggs kneeling in the remains of the glass table. He was clutching at his left arm with his right hand. Blood was pulsing steadily between his long fingers and making a pool on the glass-littered floor. The face he turned to me was so white that he looked as if he were wearing greasepaint. "What will you do, Lady?" he said.

Do? I thought. I'm a vet. I can't be expected to deal with humans! "For goodness' sake, Eggs," I snapped at him. "Stop this messing about and get me the Master! Now. This instant!"

I think he said, "And I thought you'd never tell me!" But his voice was so far from human by then it was hard to be sure. His body boiled about on the floor, surging and seething and changing color. In next to a second the thing on the floor was a huge gray wolf, with its back arched and its jaws wide in agony, pumping blood from a severed artery in its left foreleg.

At least I knew what to do with that. But before I could move, the door to the outside slid open to let in the great head and shoulders of Annie. I backed away. The look in those light, blazing eyes said: "You are not taking my mate like *she* did."

Here the chiming got into my head and proved to be the ringing of the telephone. My bedside clock said 5:55 A.M. I was quite glad to be rid of that dream as I fumbled the telephone up in the dark. "Yes?" I said, hoping I sounded as sleepy as I felt.

The voice was a light, high one, possibly a man's. "You won't know me," it said. "My name is Harrison Ovett, and I'm in charge of an experimental project involving wild animals. We have a bit of an emergency on here. One of the wolves seems to be in quite a bad way. I'm sorry to call you at such an hour, but—"

"It's my job," I said, too sleepy to be more than proud of the professional touch. "Where are you? How do I get to your project?"

I think he hesitated slightly. "It's a bit complicated to explain," he said. "Suppose I come and pick you up? I'll be outside in twenty minutes."

"Right," I said. And it was not until I put the phone down that I remembered my dream. The name was the same, I swear. I would equally swear to the voice. This is why I have spent the last twenty minutes feverishly dictating this account of my dream. If I get back safely, I'll erase it. But if I don't—well, I am not sure what anyone can do if Annie's torn my throat out, but at least someone will know what became of me. Besides, they say forewarned is forearmed. I have some idea what to expect.

ENNA HITTIMS

A nne Smith hated having mumps. She had to miss two school outings. Her face came up so long and purple that both her parents laughed at her when they were at home. And she was left alone rather a lot, because her parents could not afford to leave their jobs.

The first day was terrible. Anne's temperature went up and up, and the higher it got, the more hungry she became. By the time her father got off work early and came home, she was starving.

"But people aren't supposed to get hungry with a temperature!" Mr. Smith said, grinning at the sight of Anne's great purple face.

"I don't care. I want five sausages and two helpings of chips and lots of ketchup," said Anne. "Quickly, or I'll die!"

So Mr. Smith raced out to the chip shop. But when he came back, Anne could not open her mouth far enough to get a bite of sausage. She could not chew the chips. And the ketchup stung the inside of her face like nettles.

"I told you so," said Mr. Smith.

Anne, who was usually a most reasonable person, burst into tears and threw all the food on the floor. "I'm so hungry!" she yelled. "It's torture!" Of course it hurt to shout, too.

Mr. Smith was reasonable, too, except when he had to clean ketchup off the carpet. He lost his temper and shouted, "Do that again, and I'll spank you, mumps or not!"

"I hate you," said Anne. "I hate everything." And she sat and glowered, which is the only way to be angry with mumps.

"I think she's got grumps as well as mumps," Mrs. Smith said when she got in from work.

It did seem to be so. For the next few days, nothing pleased Anne. She tried wandering about the house—very slowly, because moving jiggled her great mauve face—looking for things to do. Nothing seemed interesting. She tried playing with Tibby, the cat, but Tibby was boring. She tried watching videos, but they were either boring or they made her laugh, and laughing hurt. She tried reading, but that was the same, and her fat, swollen chin kept getting in the way. Everything was boring. Mrs. Harvey next door had kindly agreed to come in and give Anne lunch. But it did not seem to occur to Mrs. Harvey that things like crusty pizza and stewed rhubarb are the last things you want to eat with mumps.

Anne told her parents all this when they got home. The result was that her parents stopped saying, "It's the way you feel with mumps." Instead, they said, "Oh, for heaven's sake, Anne, do stop grumbling!" every time Anne opened her mouth.

Anne took herself and her great purple face back to bed, where she lay staring at the shape of her legs under the bedclothes and hating her parents. I'm seriously ill, she thought, and nobody cares!

The next minute she had invented Enna Hittims.

It all happened in a flash, but when she thought about it later, Anne supposed it was because the shape of her legs under the bedspread looked like a landscape with two long hills in it and a green jungly valley in between. The long wrinkle running down from her left foot looked like a gorge where a river might run. Even through her crossness, Anne seemed to be wondering what it would be like to be small enough to explore those hills and that valley.

Enna Hittims was small enough. The name was Anne Smith backward, of course. But there is no way you can say "Htims" without putting in a noise between the *H* and the *t*, so Enna's second name had to be Hittims. It suited her. She was a bold and heroic lady, even if she was only an inch or so high. She was tall and slim and muscular, and she wore her raven locks cut short around her thin brown face. There was no trace of mumps about Enna Hittims, and no trace of cowardice either. Enna Hittims was born to explore and have adventures.

Enna Hittims started life on her parents' farm beside the Crease River, just below Leftoe Mountain. She was plowing their cornfield one day, when the plow turned up an old sword. Enna Hittims picked it up and swished it, and it cut through the plow. It was an enchanted sword that could cut through anything. Enna Hittims took the sword home to where her parents were lazing about and cut the kitchen table in half to show them what it could do.

"I'm leaving," she said. "I want to have adventures."

"No, you're not," said her parents. "We forbid it. We need you to do the work."

Then Enna Hittims realized that her parents were exploiting her. She cut both their heads off with the enchanted sword and set off from the farm with a small bundle of food, to look for what she might find.

In this way Enna Hittims began the most exciting and interesting kind of life. For the next few days Anne found it hard to think of anything else. She lay in bed and looked at the landscape on the bedspread and imagined adventures for Enna Hittims to go with it.

The first heroic deed Enna Hittims did was to kill a tiger at Ankle Bend. Tibby put this idea into Anne's head by coming to sleep on her bed. After that Enna Hittims climbed on up the mountain, where the landscape grew ever more wondrous. In the giant fern forest near the top of Leftoe Mountain, where

monkeys chattered and parrots screamed, Enna Hittims came
upon two more intrepid travelers, who were about to be killed
by a savage gorilla. Enna Hittims cut the gorilla's head off for
them, and the two travelers became her faithful friends. They
were called Marlene and Spike. The heroic three set off to find
the treasure guarded by the dragon on Knee Heights.

By this time, Anne was finding Enna Hittims and her friends
so interesting that she just had to get out of bed for her drawing
book and felt tips and draw pictures of their adventures. Of
course, when she got back into bed, the landscape had changed.
The green patch which had been the fern forest had got down
between Anne's feet and become the Caves of Emerald, and the
Crease River had turned into Toagara Falls. Enna Hittims and
her friends realized they were exploring an enchanted land and
took it all quite calmly. As the landscape changed every time
Anne got in and out of bed, they soon understood that a powerful magician was trying to stop them getting the treasure. Enna
Hittims vowed to conquer the magician when they had killed
the dragon.

The three friends explored all over the bedspread. Anne made
drawing after drawing of them. She no longer minded Tibby's
being so boring. While Tibby was curled up asleep on the bed,
she held still for Anne to draw her. Anne intended Tibby to be
the dragon in the end, but meanwhile, Tibby made a useful
model for all the other monsters the three heroes killed. For the
human monsters, Anne fetched snapshots of her parents and her
cousins and copied them with glaring eyes and long teeth.

Enna Hittims was easy to draw. Her bold dark face gave Anne
no trouble at all. Marlene was almost as easy, because she was
the opposite of her friend, fair and small and not very brave.
Enna Hittims often had to snap at Marlene for being so scared.
Spike was more trouble to draw. Of course he had spiky hair,
but his name really came from the enchanted spike he used as a
weapon. He was small and nimble, with a puckered face. Anne

kept getting him looking like a monkey, until she got used to drawing him. She drew and drew. Every time she got out of bed and the landscape changed, she thought of new adventures. She hardly noticed what Mrs. Harvey brought her for lunch. She hardly noticed whether her parents were in or out.

"Thank goodness!" said Mr. and Mrs. Smith.

And then disaster struck. Just before lunchtime, when Anne was all alone in the house, every one of her felt tips ran out.

"Oh, bother!" Anne wailed, almost in tears. She scribbled angrily, but even the mauve felt tip only made a pale, squeaky line. It was awful. Enna Hittims and her friends were in the middle of meeting the hermit who knew where to find the dragon. Anne was dying to draw the hermit's cave. Enna Hittims was holding her enchanted sword threateningly at the foolish hermit's throat. Anne had a photograph of Mr. Smith all ready to copy as the hermit. She was looking forward to giving him long hair and a scraggly beard and a look of utter terror.

"Oh, *bother!*" she shouted, and threw the felt tips across the room.

Tibby by now knew all about Anne in this mood. She jumped off Anne's bed and galloped for the door. Mrs. Harvey came in with Anne's lunch just then. Tibby slipped around Mrs. Harvey and ran away.

"Here you are, dear," Mrs. Harvey said, puffing rather. She put a tray down on Anne's knees. "I've done you macaroni cheese and some nice stewed apple. You can eat that, can't you?"

Anne knew Mrs. Harvey was being very kind. She smiled, in spite of her crossness, and said, "Yes, thank you."

"I should think you'd be well enough to go downstairs a bit now," Mrs. Harvey said, a little reproachfully. "The stairs are hard work." She went away, saying, "Tell your dad to pop the dishes back tonight. I'm out till then."

Anne sighed and looked back at the bedspread. To her surprise, Enna Hittims had killed the hermit during the interruption. Anne had meant the hermit to stay alive and guide the heroes to the dragon. She stared at Enna Hittims coolly wiping her enchanted sword clean on a handy tuft of cloth. "Sorry if I lost my temper," Enna Hittims was saying, "but I don't think the old fool knew a thing about that dragon."

Anne was rather shocked. She had not known that Enna Hittims was that unfeeling.

"You did quite right," said Spike. "You know, I'm beginning to wonder if that dragon exists at all."

"Me, too," answered Enna Hittims. She hitched her sword to her belt rather grimly. "And if someone's having us on—"

"Enna," Marlene interrupted, "the landscape's changed again. Over there."

The three heroes swung around and shaded their eyes with their hands to look at the tray across Anne's lap. "So it has!" said Enna Hittims. "Well done, Marlene! What is it up there?"

"A tableland," said Spike. "There are two white mountains, and one's steaming. Do you think it could be the dragon?"

"Probably only a new volcano," said Enna Hittims. "Let's go and see."

The three heroes set off along the top of Anne's right leg, walking swiftly in single file, and Anne watched them in some alarm. She did not want them climbing over her lunch while she tried to eat it.

"Go back," she said. "The dragon's going to be down by my right knee."

"What was that?" Marlene whispered nervously as she followed the other two up the slant of Anne's thigh.

"Just thunder. We're always hearing it," said Enna Hittims. "Don't whinge, Marlene."

The three heroes stood in a row with their chins on the edge of the lunch tray.

"Well, how about that!" said Enna Hittims. She pointed to the plate of macaroni cheese. "That hill of hot pipes—do you think it's an installation of some kind?"

"There could be a baby dragon in each pipe," Marlene suggested.

"What are those shiny things?" Spike wondered, pointing at the knife, fork, and spoon.

"Silver bars," Enna Hittims said. "We'll have to find an elephant and tow them away. This must be the dragon's lair. But what's that?"

The three heroes stared at the bowl of stewed apple.

"Pale yellow slush," said Spike, "with a sour smell. Dragon sick?"

"It could be some kind of gold mulch," Marlene said doubtfully. She looked carefully across the tray, searching for some clue. Her eyes went on, up the hill of Anne's body beyond. She jumped and clutched Spike's sleeve. "Look!" she whispered. "Up there!"

Spike looked. He turned quietly to Enna Hittims. "Look up, but don't be too obvious about it," he murmured. "Isn't that a giant face up there?"

Enna Hittims glanced up. She nodded. "Right. Very big and purple, with little, piggy eyes. It's some kind of giant. We'll have to kill it."

"Now look here—" Anne called out.

But the three heroes took her voice for thunder, just as they always did. Enna Hittims went on briskly laying her plans. "Marlene and Spike, you go around the tableland, one on each side, and climb up its hair. Swing over when you're above the nose and stab an eye each. I'll go in over the middle and see if I can cut its fat throat." Spike and Marlene nodded and raced away around the edges of the tray.

Anne did not wait to see if the plan worked. She picked up the tray and pushed it on top of her bedside cupboard. Then she scrambled out of bed as fast as she could go. This of course changed the landscape completely, toppling all three heroes over and burying them under mountains of sheet and blanket. Anne hoped that had done for them. It ought to have done, since they were only part of her imagination.

To give them time to smother, or vanish, or something, Anne went down to the kitchen and got herself a glass of milk. She looked for Tibby to give her some milk, too, but Tibby seemed to have gone out through her cat flap. She went back to her bedroom, hoping the heroes had gone.

They were still there. Spike was up on her pillow, whirling his spike around his head on the end of a rope. He let it fly just as Anne came in, and it stuck firmly into the edge of the tray. It was a tin tray, but the spike was magic, of course, and would stick into anything Spike wanted it to. Spike, Enna Hittims, and Marlene all took hold of the rope and heaved. The tray slid. It tipped.

"No, stop!" Anne said weakly. She had not balanced the tray properly in her hurry.

One end of the tray came down into the bed. Down slid the macaroni cheese, and down slid the stewed apple after it. The heroes saw it coming. They leaped expertly for safety up on the pillows. They were used to this kind of thing. While Anne was still staring at macaroni and apple soaking into her sheets, Spike was dashing down and rescuing his spike.

Enna Hittims walked around the marsh of stewed apple and sliced at a macaroni tube with her sword. "It's not alive," she said. "Don't just stand there, Marlene. We're going up that ramp to find that giant and finish him off. It's obviously the giant that's been changing the landscape all the time. No giant's going to do that to me!"

They started scrambling up the sloping tray. Anne hoped it

would be too slippery for them. But no. Spike used his spike to help him scramble up. Enna Hittims used her sword one-handed to hack footholds and walked up backward, dragging Marlene with her other hand and snapping, "Do come *on*, Marlene!"

Even before they were halfway up to the bedside cupboard, Anne knew that the only sensible thing to do was to pick the tray up and tip them back into the stewed apple. And then put the tray on top of them and press. But she could not bring herself to do anything so nasty. She stood and watched them climb on top of the cupboard. Enna Hittims stood with her hands on her hips, surveying the bedroom.

"We're in the giant's house now," she said confidently.

"And he'll be a mountain of cat food before long," said Spike. Marlene laughed with pleasure.

Anne ran out of the bedroom and shut the door with a slam. She ran down to the living room and stood with her hands together and her eyes shut. "Go away, all three of you!" she prayed. "Go. Disappear. Vanish. You're only made up!"

Then she went back upstairs to see if the prayer had worked. Her bedroom door was still shut, but there was some kind of purple tube sticking out from under the door. As Anne bent down to see what it was, she heard Enna Hittims's voice from behind the door. "Well, what *is* out there, Marlene?"

"A huge passage," Marlene's voice replied. The tube was the mauve felt tip with its inside taken out. It swung sideways as Anne looked. "Oh!" said Marlene. "There's a giant out there now! I can see its toes."

"Great!" said Enna Hittims. "Let's get after it." There was a burring, splintering noise. The tip of Enna Hittims's enchanted sword, together with a lot of sawdust, made a neat half circle in the bottom of the bedroom door.

Anne ran away to the bathroom and sat on the edge of the

bath, wondering what to do. She heard the voices of the three heroes out in the passage after a moment. She shut the bathroom door, very quietly. Nothing happened. After a while she felt she had better go and see what the heroes were doing.

There was a hole like a mousehole in the bottom of her bedroom door. The heroes were on their way downstairs. Anne could hear Enna Hittims saying, "Come *on,* Marlene! Just let yourself drop and Spike will catch you." They seemed to be halfway down. Anne went down cautiously to see how they were doing it. They seemed to be letting themselves down on the rope tied to Spike's magic spike. Marlene was dangling and spinning on the rope. To Anne's surprise, she was wearing a new dress of a pretty harebell blue.

"Ooh! It's so high!" she said.

"Don't be so feeble!" said Enna Hittims. "We're halfway down."

Spike was keeping guard. "There's a giant on the stairs above us," he said quietly.

Enna Hittims glanced up at Anne. "You two go on," she said. "It's only a small one. You two get down and look for the big giants, while I slice off a few of this one's toes to keep it busy."

Anne was forced to run back to the bathroom again, rather than lose her toes. Then she realized that her bedroom was safe now and went back there. It was in the most awful mess, even if you did not count the lunch in the bed. The heroes had pulled books and jigsaws and games out of the shelves. Enna Hittims had slashed Anne's piggy bank to bits with her sword, but she obviously had not thought that 50p in pence was much of a treasure, and she had cut some of the money up, too. Spike had pulled out Anne's records. She could see the scratches his spike had made, right across her favorite ones. One of them had scribbled with a mauve felt tip across most of Anne's drawings. But it was Marlene who had done the worst damage. She had cut a ragged circle out of Anne's best sweater in order to make herself her new dress.

That made Anne so angry that she almost ran downstairs. By now she hated all three heroes. Enna Hittims was bossy and bloodthirsty. Spike was a vandal. And Marlene was so awful that she deserved the way Enna Hittims ordered her about! Anne wished she had never invented them. But it was plain she was not going to get rid of them by just wishing. She was going to have to do something, however nasty that might be.

As she arrived at the bottom of the stairs, quaking but determined, there was a ringing SMASH! from the living room and the sound of smithereens pattering on the carpet. Anne knew it was the big china lamp her mother was so fond of.

The heroes came scampering around the living room door into the hall. "Too many hazards in there," Enna Hittims announced. "Now let's see. We're sure the small purple-faced giant is only a servant left on guard. Where can we go to kill the big ones when they come back?"

"The kitchen," said Spike. "They'll want to eat."

"Us, probably," Marlene quavered.

"Don't moan, Marlene," said Enna Hittims. "Right. To the kitchen!" She held her sword up and led the other two at a run around the open kitchen door.

Something in the kitchen went *ching*-BOING! and there was the glop-glop-glop of liquid running out of a bottle. "Oh, no!" said Anne. She had left the milk bottle on the floor while she was looking for Tibby. Worse still, she remembered the way Tibby always knew when there was milk on the floor. She could not let Tibby get in the way of the enchanted sword. She ran across the hall.

"My new dress is soaked!" she heard Marlene whine. Then came the sound of Tibby's cat flap opening. Marlene gasped, "A monster!"

"What a splendid one!" Enna Hittims cried ringingly. "You two guard my rear while I kill it."

By the time Anne got to the kitchen, Enna Hittims was standing in a warlike attitude facing Tibby, barring Tibby's way to the pool of milk on the floor. And Tibby, who had no kind of idea about enchanted swords, was crouching with her tail swishing, staring eagerly at Enna Hittims. It was clear she thought the hero was a new kind of mouse.

Anne charged through the kitchen and caught Tibby just as she sprang. "Oh-ho!" shouted Enna Hittims. The enchanted sword swung at Anne's right foot. Spike sprang at Anne's left foot and stabbed. Tibby struggled and clawed. But Anne hung on to Tibby in spite of it all. She ran out into the hall, kicking the kitchen door shut behind her, and did not let go of Tibby until the door was shut. Then she dropped Tibby. Tibby stood in a ruffled hump, giving Anne the look that meant they would not be on speaking terms for some time, and then stalked away upstairs.

Anne sat on the bottom stair, watching blood ooze from a round hole in her left big toe and more blood trickle from a deep cut under her right ankle. "How lucky I didn't invent them poisoned weapons!" she said. She sat and thought. Surely one ordinary-sized girl ought to be able to defeat three inch-high heroes, if she went about it the right way. She needed armor really.

She went thoughtfully up to her bedroom. Tibby was now crouched on Anne's bed, delicately picking pieces of macaroni cheese out of the stewed apple. Tibby loved cheese. She looked up at Anne with the look that meant "Stop me if you dare!"

"You eat it," said Anne. "Be my guest. Stuff yourself. It'll keep you up here out of danger." She got dressed. She put on her toughest jeans and her hard shoes and her thickest sweater and then the zip-up plastic jacket to make quite sure. She tied the covers of her drawing book around her legs to make even more sure. Then she collected a handful of shoelaces, string, and belts and picked up the tray. It had little regular notches in it where Enna Hittims had carved her footholds. Mrs. Harvey would not be pleased.

She shut her bedroom door to keep Tibby in there and went down to the living room. She stepped over the pieces of the china lamp to the dining area and fetched out the tea trolley. Then she spent quite a long time tying the tray to the front of the trolley, testing it, and tying it again. When she had it tied firmly, so that it grated along the carpet as the trolley was pushed, and nothing an inch high could possibly get under the bottom edge of the tray, Anne picked up the poker. She was ready.

She wheeled the armored trolley out through the hall. By lying on her stomach across the top of it, she managed to reach the handle of the kitchen door and open it quietly. She looked warily inside.

She was in luck. The three heroes thought they had defeated her. They were relaxing, filling their waterskins at the edge of the pool of milk. "Now remember to go for the big giants' eyes," Enna Hittims was saying. "You can hold on to their ears if they have short hair."

"No, you can't!" Anne shouted. She shoved off with one foot and sent the trolley through the pool of milk toward them. The tray raised a tidal wave in front of it as it went. The heroes had to leap back and run, or they would have been submerged. They ran across the kitchen, shouting angrily. Anne followed them with the trolley. This way and that, they ran. But the trolley was good at turning this way and that, too. Anne pushed with her foot, and pushed. Whenever the heroes tried to run to one side of the tray, she leaned over and jabbed at them with the poker to keep them in front of it. Spike's spike tinged against the tray. Enna Hittims carved several pieces off the poker. But it did no good. Within minutes, Anne had pushed and prodded and herded them up against the back door where the cat flap was. She let them hew angrily at the tray, while she leaned over and pushed the cat flap open with the poker.

"There's a way out!" squeaked Marlene.

"Stupid! It's just tempting us!" shouted Enna Hittims.

But Anne gave the heroes no choice. She held the cat flap open and shoved hard with her foot. The tray went right up against the door. The heroes were forced to leap out through the cat flap or be squashed.

"We'll get in another way!" Enna Hittims shouted angrily as the flap banged shut.

"No, you won't!" said Anne. She left the trolley pushed against the door, and she overturned the kitchen table and pushed that up against the back of the trolley to keep it there.

She was just setting off to make sure all the windows were shut when she heard a car outside. It was the unmistakable, growly sound of her father turning the car around in the road before he backed down into the garage. A glance at the kitchen clock showed Anne that he was back almost two hours early.

"I can't let them stab his eyes!" she gasped. She raced through the hall, her head full of visions of the heroes standing on the garden wall and climbing up Mr. Smith as he walked back around from the garage. She dragged the front door open and made warning gestures with the poker.

Mr. Smith smiled at her through the back window of the car. The car was already swinging round backward into the driveway. Anne stood where she was, with the poker raised. She held her breath. The heroes were standing about halfway up the drive. Marlene was pointing at the car and gasping as usual. "Another monster!"

"Go for its big black feet!" Enna Hittims shouted, and she led the three heroes at a run toward the car.

Mr. Smith never saw them. He backed briskly down the drive. Halfway there, the heroes saw the danger. Marlene screamed, and they all turned and ran the other way. But the car, even slowing down, was moving far faster than they could run. Anne watched the big, black, zigzag-patterned tire roll over on top of them. There was the tiniest possible crunching. Much as she hated the heroes by now, Anne let her breath out with a shudder.

Before Anne could lower the poker, there was a sharp hiss. The enchanted sword, and perhaps the magic spike, too, could still do damage. Mr. Smith jumped out of the car. Anne ran across the lawn, and they both watched the right-hand back tire sink into a flat squashiness.

Mr. Smith looked ruefully from the tire to Anne's face. "Your face has gone down, too," he said. "Did you know?"

"*Has* it?" Anne put up her hand to feel. The mumps were now only two small lumps on either side of her chin.

While she was feeling them, her father turned and got something out of the car. "Here you are," he said. He passed her a fat new drawing book and a large pack of felt tips. "I knew you were going to run out of drawing things today."

Anne looked at the rows of different colors and the thick book of paper. She knew her father hated going to the drawing shop. There was never anywhere to park, and he always got a parking ticket. But he had gone there specially and then come home early to give them to her. "Thanks!" she said. "Er—I'm afraid there's rather a mess indoors."

Mr. Smith smiled cheerfully. "Then isn't it lucky you're so much better?" he said. "You can tidy up while I'm putting the spare wheel on."

It seemed fair, Anne thought. She turned toward the house, wondering where to start. The macaroni, the china lamp, or the milk? She looked down at the pack of felt tips while she tried to decide. They were a different make from the old lot. That was a good thing. She was fairly sure that it was her drawings that had brought Enna Hittims and her friends to life like that. The old felt tips would not have been called Magic Markers for nothing.

THE GIRL WHO
LOVED THE SUN

There was a girl called Phega who became a tree. Stories from the ancient times when Phega lived would have it that when women turned into trees, it was always under duress, because a god was pursuing them, but Phega turned into a tree voluntarily. She did it from the moment she entered her teens. It was not easy, and it took a deal of practice, but she kept at it. She would go into the fields beyond the manor house where she lived, and there she would put down roots, spread her arms, and say, "For you I shall spread out my arms." Then she would become a tree.

She did this because she was in love with the sun. The people who looked after her when she was a child told her that the sun loved the trees above all other living things. Phega concluded that this must be so from the way most trees shed their leaves in winter when the sun was unable to attend to them very much. As Phega could not remember a time when the sun had not been more to her than mother, father, or life itself, it followed that she had to become a tree.

At first she was not a very good tree. The trunk of her tended to bulge at hips and breast and was usually an improbable brown color. The largest number of branches she could achieve was four or five at the most. These stood out at unconvincing angles and grew large, pallid leaves in a variety of shapes. She strove with these defects valiantly, but for a long time it always seemed that when she got her trunk to look more natural, her branches were fewer and more misshapen, and when she grew halfway decent branches, either her trunk relapsed or her leaves were too large or too yellow.

"Oh, sun"—she sighed—"do help me to be more pleasing to you." Yet it seemed unlikely that the sun was even attending to her. "But he will!" Phega said, and driven by hope and yearning, she continued to stand in the field, striving to spread out more plausible branches. Whatever shape they were, she could still revel in the sun's impartial warmth on them and in the searching strength of her roots reaching into the earth. Whether the sun was attending or not, she knew the deep peace of a tree's long, wordless thoughts. The rain was pure delight to her, instead of the necessary evil it was to other people, and the dew was a marvel.

The following spring, to her delight, she achieved a reasonable shape, with a narrow, lissome trunk and a cloud of spread branches, not unlike a fruiting tree. "Look at me, sun," she said. "Is this the kind of tree you like?"

The sun glanced down at her. Phega stood at that instant between hope and despair. It seemed that he attended to the wordless words.

But the sun passed on, beaming, not unkindly, to glance at the real apple trees that stood on the slope of the hill.

I need to be different in some way, Phega said to herself.

She became a girl again and studied the apple trees. She watched them put out big pale buds and saw how the sun drew those buds open to become leaves and white flowers. Choking with the hurt of rejection, she saw the sun dwelling lovingly on those flowers, which made her think at first that flowers were what she needed. Then she saw that the sun drew those flowers on, quite ruthlessly, until they died, and that what came after were green blobs that turned into apples.

"Now I know what I need," she said.

It took a deal of hard work, but the following spring she was able to say, "Look at me, sun. For you I shall hold out my arms budded with growing things," and spread branches full of white blossom that she was prepared to force on into fruit.

This time, however, the sun's gaze fell on her only in the way it fell on all living things. She was very dejected. Her yearning for the sun to love her grew worse.

"I still need to be different in some way," she said.

That year she studied the sun's ways and likings as she had never studied them before. In between she was a tree. Her yearning for the sun had grown so great that when she was in human form, it was as if she were less than half alive. Her parents and other human company were shadowy to her. Only when she was a tree with her arms spread to the sunlight did she feel she was truly in existence.

As that year took its course, she noticed that the place the sun first touched unfailingly in the morning was the top of the hill beyond the apple trees. And it was the place where he lingered last at sunset. Phega saw this must be the place the sun loved best. So, though it was twice as far from the manor, Phega went daily to the top of that hill and took root there. This meant that she had an hour more of the sun's warm company to spread her boughs into, but the situation was not otherwise as good as the fields. The top of the hill was very dry. When she put down roots, the soil was thin and tasted peculiar. And there was always a wind up there. Phega found she grew bent over and rather stunted.

"But what more can I do?" she said to the sun. "For you I shall spread out my arms, budded with growing things, and root within the ground you warm, accepting what that brings."

The sun gave no sign of having heard, although he continued to linger on the top of the hill at the beginning and end of each day. Phega would walk home in the twilight considering how she might grow roots that were adapted to the thin soil and pondering ways and means to strengthen her trunk against the wind. She walked slightly bent over and her skin was pale and withered.

Up till now Phega's parents had indulged her and not interfered. Her mother said, "She's very young." Her father agreed and said, "She'll get over this obsession with rooting herself in time." But when they saw her looking pale and withered and walking with a stoop, they felt the time had come to intervene. They said to one another, "She's old enough to marry now, and she's ruining her looks."

The next day they stopped Phega before she left the manor on her way to the hill. "You must give up this pining and rooting," her mother said to her. "No girl ever found a husband by being out in all weathers like this."

And her father said, "I don't know what you're after with this tree nonsense. I mean, we can all see you're very good at it, but it hasn't got much bearing on the rest of life, has it? You're our only child, Phega. You have the future of the manor to consider. I want you married to the kind of man I can trust to look after the place when I'm gone. That's not the kind of man who's going to want to marry a tree."

Phega burst into tears and fled away across the fields and up the hill.

"Oh, dear!" her father said guiltily. "Did I go too far?"

"Not at all," said her mother. "I would have said it if you hadn't. We must start looking for a husband for her. Find the right man, and this nonsense will slide out of her head from the moment she claps eyes on him."

It happened that Phega's father had to go away on business, anyway. He agreed to extend his journey and look for a suitable husband for Phega while he was away. His wife gave him a good deal of advice on the subject, ending with a very strong directive not to tell any prospective suitor that Phega had this odd habit of becoming a tree—at least not until the young man was safely proved to be interested in marriage, anyway. And as soon as her husband was away from the manor, she called two servants she could trust and told them to follow Phega and watch how she turned into a tree. "For it must be a process we can put a stop to somehow," she said, "and if you can find out how we can stop her for good, so much the better."

Phega, meanwhile, rooted herself breathlessly into the shallow soil at the top of the hill. "Help me," she called out to the sun. "They're talking of marrying me and the only one I love is you!"

The sun pushed aside an intervening cloud and considered her with astonishment. "Is this why you so continually turn into a tree?" he said.

Phega was too desperate to consider the wonder of actually, at last, talking to the sun. She said, "All I do, I do in the remote, tiny hope of pleasing you and causing you to love me as I love you."

"I had no idea," said the sun, and he added, not unkindly, "but I do love everything according to its nature, and your nature is human. I might admire you for so skillfully becoming a tree, but that is, when all is said and done, only an imitation of a tree. It follows that I love you better as a human." He beamed and was clearly about to pass on.

Phega threw herself down on the ground, half woman and half tree, and wept bitterly, thrashing her branches and rolling back and forth. "But I love you," she cried out. "You are the light of the world, and I love you. I *have* to be a tree because then I have no heart to ache for you, and even as a tree I ache at night because you aren't there. Tell me what I can do to make you love me."

The sun paused. "I do not understand your passion," he said. "I have no wish to hurt you, but this is the truth: I cannot love you as an imitation of a tree."

A small hope came to Phega. She raised the branches of her head. "Could you love me if I stopped pretending to be a tree?"

"Naturally," said the sun, thinking this would appease her. "I would love you according to your nature, human woman."

"Then I make a bargain with you," said Phega. "I will stop pretending and you will love me."

"If that is what you want," said the sun, and went on his way.

Phega shook her head free of branches and her feet from the ground and sat up, brooding, with her chin on her hands. That was how her mother's servants found her and watched her warily from among the apple trees. She sat there for hours. She had bargained with the sun as a person might bargain for her very life, out of the desperation of her love, and she needed to work out a plan to back her bargain with. It gave her slight shame that she was trying to trap such a being as the sun, but she knew that was not going to stop her. She was beyond shame.

There is no point imitating something that already exists, she said to herself, because that is pretending to be that thing. I will have to be some kind that is totally new.

Phega came down from the hill and studied trees again. Because of the hope her bargain had given her, she studied in a new way, with passion and depth, all the time her father was away. She ranged far afield to the forests in the valleys beyond the manor, where she spent days among the trees, standing still as a tree, but in human shape—which puzzled her mother's servants exceedingly—listening to the creak of their growth and every rustle of every leaf, until she knew them as trees knew other trees and comprehended the abiding restless stillness of them. The entire shape of a tree against the sky became open to her, and she came to know all their properties. Trees had power. Willows had pithy centers and grew fast; they caused sleep. Elder was pithy, too; it could give powerful protection but had a touchy nature and should be treated politely. But the oak and the ash, the giant trees that held their branches closest to the sun's love, had the greatest power of all. Oak was constancy, and ash was change. Phega studied these two longest and most respectfully.

"I need the properties of both these," she said.

She carried away branches of leafing twigs to study as she walked home, noting the join of twig to twig and the way the leaves were fastened on. Evergreens impressed her by the way they kept leaves for the sun even in winter, but she was soon sure they did it out of primitive parsimony. Oaks, on the other hand, had their leaves tightly knotted on by reason of their strength.

"I shall need the same kind of strength," Phega said.

As autumn drew on, the fruiting trees preoccupied her, since it was clear that it was growth and fruition the sun seemed most to love. They all, she saw, partook of the natures of both oaks and elders, even hawthorn, rowan, and hazel. Indeed, many of them were related to the lowlier bushes and fruiting plants, but the giant trees that the sun most loved were more exclusive in their pedigrees.

"Then I shall be like the oak," Phega said, "but bear better fruit."

Winter approached, and trees were felled for firewood. Phega was there, where the foresters were working, anxiously inspecting the rings of the sawn trunk and interrogating the very sawdust. This mystified the servants who were following her. They asked the foresters if they had any idea what Phega was doing.

The foresters shook their heads and said, "She is not quite sane, but we know she is very wise."

The servants had to be content with this. At least after that they had an easier time, for Phega was mostly at home in the manor examining the texture of the logs for the fires. She studied the bark on the outside and then the longwise grains and the roundwise rings of the interior, and she came to an important conclusion: an animal stopped growing when it had attained a certain shape, but a tree did not.

"I see now," she said, "that I have by no means finished growing." And she was very impatient because winter had put a stop to all growth, so that she had to wait for spring to study its nature.

In the middle of winter her father came home. He had found the perfect husband for Phega and was anxious to tell Phega and her mother all about the man. This man was a younger son of a powerful family, he said, and he had been a soldier for some years, during which time he had distinguished himself considerably and gained a name for sense and steadiness. Now he was looking for a wife to marry and settle down with. Though he was not rich, he was not poor either, and he was on good terms with the wealthier members of his family. It was, said Phega's father, a most desirable match.

Phega barely listened to all this. She went away to look at the latest load of logs before her father had finished speaking. He may not ever come here, she said to herself, and if he does, he will see I am not interested and go away again.

"Did I say something wrong?" her father asked her mother. "I had hoped to show her that the man has advantages that far outweigh the fact that he is not in his first youth."

"No—it's just the way she is," said Phega's mother. "Have you invited the man here?"

"Yes, he is coming in the spring," her father said. "His name is Evor. Phega will like him."

Phega's mother was not entirely sure of this. She called the servants she had set to follow Phega to her privately and asked them what they had found out. "Nothing," they said. "We think she has given up turning into a tree. She has never so much as put forth a root while we are watching her."

"I hope you are right," said Phega's mother. "But I want you

to go on watching her, even more carefully than before. It is
now extremely important that we know how to stop her becoming a tree if she ever threatens to do so."

The servants sighed, knowing they were in for another dull
and difficult time. And they were not mistaken because, as soon
as the first snowdrops appeared, Phega was out in the countryside studying the way things grew. As far as the servants were
concerned, she would do nothing but sit or stand for hours
watching a bud, or a tree, or a nest of mice or birds. As far as
Phega was concerned, it was a long fascination as she divined
how cells multiplied again and again and at length discovered
that while animals took food from solid things, plants took their
main food from the sun himself. "I think that may be the secret
at last," she said.

This puzzled the servants, but they reported it to Phega's
mother all the same. Her answer was, "I *thought* so. Be ready to
bring her home the instant she shows a root or a shoot."

The servants promised to do this, but Phega was not ready
yet. She was busy watching the whole course of spring growth
transform the forest. So it happened that Evor arrived to meet
his prospective bride and Phega was not there. She had not even
noticed that everyone in the manor was preparing a feast in
Evor's honor. Her parents sent messengers to the forest to fetch
her, while Evor first kicked his heels for several hours in the hall
and finally, to their embarrassment, grew impatient and went
out into the yard. There he wondered whether to order his
horse and leave.

I conclude from this delay, he said to himself, that the girl is
not willing, and one thing I do not want is a wife I have to force.
Nevertheless, he did not order his horse. Though Phega's parents had been at pains to keep from him any suggestion that
Phega was not as other girls were, he had been unable to avoid
hearing rumors on the way. For by this time Phega's fame was

considerable. The first gossip he heard, when he was farthest away, was that his prospective bride was a witch. This he had taken for envious persons' way of describing wisdom and pressed on. As he came nearer, rumor had it that she was very wise, and he felt justified—though the latest rumor he had heard, when he was no more than ten miles from the manor, was that Phega was at least a trifle mad. But each rumor came accompanied by statements about Phega's appearance which were enough to make him tell himself that it was too late to turn back, anyway. This kept him loitering in the yard. He wanted to set eyes on her himself.

He was still waiting when Phega arrived, walking in through the gate quickly but rather pensively. It was a gray day, with the sun hidden, and she was sad. But, she told herself, I may as well see this suitor and tell him there was no point in his coming and get it over with. She knew her parents were responsible and did not blame the man at all.

Evor looked at her as she came and knew that rumor had understated her looks. The time Phega had spent studying had improved her health and brought her from girl to young woman. She was beautiful. Evor saw that her hair was the color of beer when you hold a glass of it to the light. She was wearing a dress of smooth silver-gray material which showed that her body under it when she moved was smooth-muscled and sturdy—and he liked sturdy women. Her overgarment was a curious light, bright green and floated away from her arms, revealing them to be very round and white. When he looked at her face, which was both round and long, he saw beauty there, but he also saw that she was very wise. Her eyes were gray. He saw a wildness there contained by the deep calm of long, long thought and a capacity to drink in knowledge. He was awed. He was lost.

Phega, for her part, tore her thoughts from many hours of standing longing among the great trees and saw a wiry man of slightly over middle height, who had a bold face with a keen stare to it. She saw he was not young. There was gray to his beard—which always grew more sparsely than he would have liked, though he had combed it carefully for the occasion—and some gray in his hair, too. She noticed his hair particularly because he had come to the manor in light armor, to show his status as a soldier and a commander, but he was carrying his helmet politely in the crook of his arm. His intention was to show himself as a polished man of the world. But Phega saw him as iron-colored all over. He made her think of an ax, except that he seemed to have such a lot of hair. She feared he was brutal.

Evor said, "My lady!" and added as a very awkward afterthought, "I came to marry you." As soon as he had said this, it struck him as so wrong and presumptuous a thing to say to a woman like this one that he hung his head and stared at her feet, which were bare and, though beautiful, stained green with the grass she had walked through. The sight gave him courage. He thought that those feet were human after all, so it followed that the rest of her was, and he looked up at her eyes again. "What a thing to say!" he said.

He smiled in a flustered way. Phega saw that he was somewhat snaggle-toothed, not to speak of highly diffident in spite of his gray and military appearance, and possibly in awe of her. She could not see how he could be in awe of her, but his uneven teeth made him a person to her. Of a sudden he was not just the man her parents had procured for her to marry, but another person like her, with feelings like those Phega had herself. Good gods! she thought, in considerable surprise. This is a person I could maybe love after all, if it were not for the sun. And she told him politely that he was very welcome.

They went indoors together and presently sat down to the feast. There Evor got over his awe a little, enough to attempt to talk to Phega. And Phega, knowing he had feelings to be hurt, answered the questions he asked and asked things in return. The result was that before long, to the extreme delight of Phega's parents, they were talking of his time at war and of her knowledge and laughing together as if they were friends—old friends. Evor's wonder and joy grew. Long before the feast was over, he knew he could never love any other woman now. The effect of Phega on him was like a physical tie, half glorious, half painful, that bound him to respond to every tiny movement of her hand and every flicker of her lashes.

Phega found—and her surprise increased—that she was comfortable with Evor. But however amicably they talked, it was still as if she was only half alive in the sun's absence—though it was an easy half life—and, as the evening wore on, she felt increasingly confined and trapped. At first she assumed that this feeling was simply due to her having spent so much of the past year out of doors. She was so used to having nothing but the sky with the sun in it over her head that she often did find the manor roof confining. But now it was like a cage over her head. And she realized that her growing liking for Evor was causing it.

If I don't take care, she said to herself, I shall forget the bargain I made with the sun and drift into this human contract. It is almost too late already. I must act at once.

Thinking this, she said her good-nights and went away to sleep.

Evor remained, talking jubilantly with Phega's parents. "When I first saw her," he said, "I thought things were hopeless. But now I think I have a chance. I think she likes me."

Phega's father agreed, but Phega's mother said, "I'm sure she *likes* you all right, but—I caught a look in her eye—this may not be enough to make her marry you."

Saying this, Phega's mother touched on something Evor had sensed and feared himself. His jubilation turned ashy; indeed, he felt as if the whole world had been taken by drought; there was no moisture or virtue in it anywhere from pole to pole. "What more can I do?" he said, low and slow.

"Let me tell you something," said Phega's mother.

"Yes," Phega's father broke in eagerly. "Our daughter has a strange habit of—"

"She is," Phega's mother interrupted swiftly, "under an enchantment which we are helpless to break. Only a man who truly loves her can break it."

Hope rose in Evor, as violent as Phega's hope when she bargained with the sun. "Tell me what to do," he said.

Phega's mother considered all the reports her servants had brought her. So far as she knew, Phega had never once turned into a tree all the time her father was away. It was possible she had lost the art. This meant that with luck, Evor need never know the exact nature of her daughter's eccentricity. "Sometime soon," she said, "probably at dawn, my daughter will be compelled by the enchantment to leave the manor. She will go to the forest or the hill. She may be compelled to murmur words to herself. You must follow her when she goes, and as soon as you see her standing still, you must take her in your arms and kiss her. In this way you will break the spell, and she will become your faithful wife ever after." And, Phega's mother told herself, this was very likely what would happen. For, she thought, as soon as he kisses her, my daughter will discover that there are certain pleasures to be had from behaving naturally. Then we can all be comfortable again.

"I shall do exactly what you say," said Evor, and he was so uplifted with hope and gratitude that his face was nearly handsome.

All that night he kept watch. He could not have slept, anyway. Love roared in his ears, and longing choked him. He went over and over the things Phega had said and each individual beauty of her face and body as she said these things, and when, in the dawn, he saw her stealing through the hall to the door, there was a moment when he could not move. She was even more lovely than he remembered.

Phega softly unbarred the door and crossed the yard to unbar the gate. Evor pulled himself together and followed. They walked out across the fields in the white time before sunrise, Phega pacing very upright, with her eyes on the sky where the sun would appear, and Evor stealing after. He softly took off his armor piece by piece as he followed her and laid it down carefully in case it should clatter and alarm her.

Up the hill Phega went, where she stood like one entranced, watching the gold rim of the sun come up. And such was Evor's awe that he loitered a little in the apple trees, admiring her as she stood.

"Now," Phega said, "I have come to fulfill my bargain, sun, since I fear this is the last time I shall truly want to." What she did then, she had given much thought to. It was not the way she had been accustomed to turn into a tree before. It was far more thorough. For she put down careful roots, driving each of her toes downward and outward and then forcing them into a network of fleshy cables to make the most of the thin soil at the top of the hill. "Here," she said, "I root within the soil you warm."

Evor saw the ground rise and writhe and low branches grow from her insteps to bury themselves also. "Oh, no!" he cried out. "Your feet were beautiful as they were!" And he began to climb the hill toward her.

Phega frowned, concentrating on the intricacy of feathery rootlets. "But they were not the way I wanted them," she said, and she wondered vaguely why he was there. But by then she was putting forth her greatest effort, which left her little attention to spare. Slowly, once her roots were established, she began to coat them with bark before insects could damage them. At the same time, she set to work on her trunk, growing swiftly, grain by growing grain. "Increased by yearly rings," she murmured.

As Evor advanced, he saw her body elongate, coating itself with mat pewter-colored bark as it grew, until he could barely pick out the outline of limbs and muscles inside it. It was like watching a death. "Don't!" he said. "Why are you *doing* this? You were lovely before!"

"I was like all human women," Phega answered, resting before her next great effort. "But when I am finished, I shall be a wholly new kind of tree." Having said that, she turned her attention to the next stage, which she was expecting to enjoy. Now she stretched up her arms, and the hair of her head, yearning into the warmth of the climbing sun, and made it all into limblike boughs, which she coated like the rest of her, carefully, with dark silver bark. "For you I shall hold out my arms," she said.

Evor saw her, tree-shaped and twice as tall as himself, and cried out, "Stop!" He was afraid to touch her in this condition. He knelt at her roots in despair.

"I can't stop now," Phega told him gently. She was gathering herself for her final effort, and her mind was on that, though the tears she heard breaking his voice did trouble her a little. She put that trouble out of her head. This was the difficult part. She had already elongated every large artery of her body, to pass through her roots and up her trunk and into her boughs. Now she concentrated on lifting her veins, and every nerve with them, without disturbing the rest, out to the ends of her branches, out and up, up and out, into a mass of living twigs, fine-growing and close as her own hair. It was impossible. It hurt—she had not thought it would hurt so much—but she was lifting, tearing her veins, thrusting her nerve ends with them, first into the innumerable fine twigs, then into even further particles to make long, sharp buds.

Evor looked up as he crouched and saw the great tree surging and thrashing above him. He was appalled at the effort. In the face of this gigantic undertaking he knew he was lost and forgotten, and besides, it was presumptuous to interfere with such willing agony. He saw her strive and strive again to force those sharp buds open. "If you must be a tree," he shouted above the din of her lashing branches, "take me with you somehow, at least!"

"Why should you want that?" Phega asked with wooden lips that had not yet quite closed, just where her main boughs parted.

Evor at last dared to clasp the trunk with its vestigial limbs showing. He shed tears on the gray bark. "Because I love you. I want to be with you."

Trying to see him forced her buds to unfurl, because that was where her senses now were. They spread with myriad shrill agonies, like teeth cutting, and she thought it had killed her, even while she was forcing further nerves and veins to the undersides of all her pale viridian leaves. When it was done, she was all alive and raw in the small hairs on the undersides of those leaves and in the symmetrical ribs of vein on the shiny upper sides, but she could sense Evor crouching at her roots now. She was grateful to him for forcing her to the necessary pain. Her agony responded to his. He was a friend. He had talked of love, and she understood that. She retained just enough of the strength it had taken to change to alter him, too, to some extent, though not enough to bring him beyond the animal kingdom. The last of her strength was reserved for putting forth small pear-shaped fruit covered with wiry hairs, each containing four triangular nuts. Then, before the wooden gap that was her mouth had entirely closed, she murmured, "Budding with growing things."

She rested for a while, letting the sun harden her leaves to a dark shiny green and ripen her fruit a little. Then she cried wordlessly to the sun, "Look! Remember our bargain. I am an entirely new kind of tree—as strong as an oak, but I bear fruit that everything can eat. Love me. Love me now!" Proudly she shed some of her three-cornered nuts onto the hilltop,

"I see you," said the sun. "This is a lovely tree, but I am not sure what you expect me to do with you."

"Love me!" she cried.

"I do," said the sun. "There is no change in me. The only difference is that I now feed you more directly than I feed that animal at your feet. It is the way I feed all trees. There is nothing else I can do."

Phega knew the sun was right and that her bargain had been her own illusion. It was very bitter to her; but she had made a change that was too radical to undo now, and besides, she was discovering that trees do not feel things very urgently. She settled back for a long, low-key sort of contentment, rustling her leaves about to make the best of the sun's heat on them. It was like a sigh.

After a while a certain activity among her roots aroused a mild arboreal curiosity in her. With senses that were rapidly atrophying, she perceived a middle-sized iron-gray animal with a sparse bristly coat, which was diligently applying its long snout to the task of eating her three-cornered nuts. The animal was decidedly snaggle-toothed. It was lean and had a sharp corner to the center of its back, as if that was all that remained of a wiry man's military bearing. It seemed to sense her attention, for it began to rub itself affectionately against her gray trunk, which still showed vestiges of rounded legs within it.

Ah, well, thought the tree, and considerately let fall another shower of beech mast for it.

That was long ago. They say that Phega still stands on the hill. She is one of the beech trees that stand on the hill that always holds the last rays of the sun, but so many of the trees in that wood are so old that there is no way to tell which one she is. All the trees show vestiges of limbs in their trunks, and all are given at times to inexplicable thrashings in their boughs, as if in memory of the agony of Phega's transformation. In the autumn their leaves turn the color of Phega's hair and often fall only in spring, as though they cling harder than most leaves in honor of the sun.

There is nothing to eat their nuts now. The wild boar vanished from there centuries ago, though the name stayed. The maps usually call the place Boar's Hill.

DRAGON RESERVE,
HOME EIGHT

Where to begin? Neal and I had had a joke for years about a little green van coming to carry me off—this was when I said anything more than usually mad—and now it was actually happening. Mother and I stood at my bedroom window, watching the van bouncing up the track between the dun green hills, and neither of us smiled. It wasn't a farm van, and most of our neighbors visit on horseback, anyway. Before long we could see it was dark green with a silver dragon insigne on the side.

"It is the Dragonate," Mother said. "Siglin, there's nothing I can do." It astonished me to hear her say that. Mother only comes up to my shoulder, but she held her land and our household, servants, Neal and me, and all three of her husbands, in a hand like iron, *and* she drove out to plow or harvest if one of my fathers was ill. "They said the dragons would take you," she said. "I should have seen. You think Orm informed on you?"

"I know he did," I said. "It was my fault for going into the Reserve."

"I'll blood an ax on him," Mother said, "one of these days. But I can't do it over this. The neighbors would say he was quite right." The van was turning between the stone walls of the farmyard now. Chickens were squirting and flapping out of its way, and our sheepdog pups were barking their heads off. I could see Neal up on the washhouse roof watching yearningly. It's a good place to watch from because you can hide behind the chimney. Mother saw Neal, too. "Siglin," she said, "don't let on Neal knows about you."

"No," I said. "Nor you either."

"Say as little as you can, and wear the old blue dress; it makes you look younger," Mother said, turning toward the door. "You might just get off. Or they might just have come about something else," she added. The van was stopping outside the front door now, right underneath my window. "I'd best go and greet them," Mother said, and hurried downstairs.

While I was forcing my head through the blue dress, I heard heavy boots on the steps and a crashing knock at the door. I shoved my arms into the sleeves, in too much of a hurry even to feel indignant about the dress. It makes me look about twelve, and I am nearly grown up! At least, I was fourteen quite a few weeks ago now. But Mother was right. If I looked too immature to have awakened, they might not question me too hard. I hurried to the head of the stairs while I tied my hair with a childish blue ribbon. I knew they had come for me, but I had to *see*.

They were already inside when I got there, a whole line of tall men tramping down the stone hallway in the half dark, and Mother was standing by the closed front door as if they had swept her aside. What a lot of them, just for me! I thought. I got a weak, sour feeling and could hardly move for horror. The man at the front of the line kept opening the doors all down the hallway, calm as you please, until he came to the main parlor at the end. "This room will do nicely," he said. "Out you get, you." And my oldest father, Timas, came shuffling hurriedly out in his slippers, clutching a pile of accounts and looking scared and worried. I saw Mother fold her arms. She always does when she is angry.

Another of them turned to Mother. "We'll speak to you first," he said, "and your daughter after that. Then we want the rest of the household. Don't any of you try to leave." And they went into the parlor with Mother and shut the door.

They hadn't even bothered to guard the doors. They just assumed we would obey them. I was shaking as I walked back to my room, but it was not terror anymore. It was rage. I mean, we have all been brought up to honor the Dragonate. They are the cream of the men of the Ten Worlds. They are supposed to be gallant and kind and dedicated and devote their lives to keeping us safe from Thrallers, not to speak of maintaining justice, law, and order all over the Ten Worlds. Dragonate men swear that oath of Alienation, which means they can never have homes or families like ordinary people. Up to then I'd felt sorry for them for that. They give up so much. But now I saw they felt it gave them the right to behave as if the rest of us were not real people. To walk in as if they owned our house. To order Timas out of his own parlor. Oh, I was angry!

I don't know how long Mother was in the parlor. I was so angry it felt like seconds until I heard flying feet and Neal hurried into my room. "They want you now."

I stood up and took some of my anger out on poor Neal. I said, "Do you still want to join the Dragonate? Swear that stupid oath? Behave like you own the Ten Worlds?"

It was mean. Neal looked at the floor. "They said straightaway," he said. Of course he wanted to join. Every boy does, particularly on Sveridge, where women own most of the land. I swept down the stairs, angrier than ever. All the doors in the hallway were open, and our people were standing in them, staring. The two housemen were at the dining room door, the cattlewomen and two farmhands were looking out of the kitchen, and the stableboy and the second shepherd were craning out of the pantry. I thought, They still will be my people someday! I refuse to be frightened! My fathers were in the doorway of the bookroom. Donal and Yan were in work clothes and had obviously rushed in without taking their boots off. I gave them what I hoped was a smile, but only Timas smiled back. They all know! I thought as I opened the parlor door.

There were only five of them, sitting facing me across our best table. Five was enough. All of them stood up as I came in. The room seemed full of towering green uniforms. It was not at all what I expected. For one thing, the media always show the Dragonate as fair and dashing and handsome, and none of these were. For another, the media had led me to expect uniforms with big silver panels. These were all plain green, and four of them had little silver stripes on one shoulder.

"Are you Sigrid's daughter, Siglin?" asked the one who had opened all the doors. He was a bleached, pious type like my father Donal, and his hair was dust color.

"Yes," I said rudely. "Who are you? Those aren't Dragonate uniforms."

"Camerati, Lady," said one who was brown all over with wriggly hair. He was young, younger than my father Yan, and he smiled cheerfully, like Yan does. But he made my stomach go cold. Camerati are the crack force, cream of the Dragonate. They say a man has to be a genius even to be considered for it.

"Then what are you doing here?" I said. "And why are you all standing up?"

The one in the middle, obviously the chief one, said, "We always stand up when a lady enters the room. And we are here because we were on a tour of inspection at Holmstad, anyway, and there was a Slaver scare on this morning. So we offered to take on civic duties for the regular Dragonate. Now if that answers your questions, let me introduce us all." He smiled, too, which twisted his white, crumpled face like a demon mask. "I am Lewin, and I'm Updriten here. On your far left is Driten Palino, our recorder." This was the pious type, who nodded. "Next to him is Driten Renick of Law Wing." Renick was elderly and iron-gray, with one of those necks that look like a chicken's leg. He just stared. "Underdriten Terens is on my left, my aide and witness." That was brown-and-wriggly. "And beyond him is Cadet Alectis, who is traveling with us to Home Nine."

Alectis looked a complete baby, only a year older than I was, with pink cheeks and sandy hair. He and Terens both bowed and smiled so politely that I nearly smiled back. Then I realized that they were treating me as if I were a visitor. In my own home! I bowed freezingly, the way Mother usually does to Orm.

"Please sit down, Siglin," Lewin said politely.

I nearly didn't, because that might keep them standing up, too. But they were all so tall I'd already got a crick in my neck. So I sat grandly on the chair they'd put ready facing the table. "Thank you," I said. "You are a very kind host, Updriten Lewin." To my great joy, Alectis went bright red at that, but the other four simply sat down, too. Pious Palino took up a memo block and poised his fingers over its keys. This seemed to be in case the recorder in front of Lewin went wrong. Lewin set that going. Wriggly Terens leaned over and passed me another little square box.

"Keep this in your hand," he said, "or your answers may not come out clearly."

I caught the words *lie detector* from his wriggly head as clearly as if he had said them aloud. I don't think I showed how very scared I was, but my hand made the box wet almost straightaway.

"Court is open," Lewin said to the recorder. "Presiding Updriten Lewin." He gave a string of numbers and then said, "First hearing starts on charges against Siglin, of Upland Holding, Wormstow, North Sveridge on Home Eight, accused of being heg and heg concealing its nature. Questions begin. Siglin, are you clear what being heg is?" He crumpled one eyebrow upward at me.

"No," I said. After all, no one has told me in so many words. It's just a thing people whisper and shudder at.

"Then you'd better understand this," Lewin said. He really was the ugliest and most outlandish of the five. Dragonate men are never posted to the world of their birth, and I thought Lewin must come from one a long way off. His hair was black, so black it had blue lights, but, instead of being dark all over to match it, like wriggly Terens, he was a lot whiter than I was, and his eyes were a most piercing blue, almost the color they make the sky on the media. "If the charges are proved," he said, "you face death by beheading since that is the only form of execution a heg cannot survive. Renick—"

Elderly Renick swept sourly in before Lewin had finished speaking. "The law defines a heg as one with human form who is not human. Medical evidence of brain pattern or nerve and muscle deviations is required prior to execution, but for a first hearing it is enough to establish that the subject can perform one or more of the following: mind reading; kindling fire or moving objects at a distance; healing or killing by the use of the mind alone; surviving shooting, drowning, or suffocation; or enslaving or otherwise afflicting the mind of a beast or human."

He had the kind of voice that bores you, anyway. I thought, Great gods! I don't think I can do half those things! Maybe I looked blank. Palino stopped clicking his memo block to say, "It's very important to understand why these creatures must be stamped out. They can make people into puppets in just the same way that the Slavers can. Foul." Actually I think he was explaining to Alectis. Alectis nodded humbly. Palino said, definitely to me, "Slavers do it with those V-shaped collars. You must have seen them on the media. Quite foul."

"We call them Thrallers," I said. Foul or not, I thought, I'm the only one of me I've got! I can't help being made the way I am.

Lewin flapped his hand to shut Palino up, and Renick went on again. "A heg is required by law to give itself up for execution. Any normal person who knowingly conceals a heg is likewise liable for execution." Now I knew why Mother had told me to keep Neal out of it.

Then it seemed to be Palino's turn. He said, "Personal details follow. How old are you, er, Sigrun?"

"Sig*lin*," I said. "Fourteen last month."

Renick stretched out his chicken neck. "In this court's opinion, subject is old enough to have awakened as heg." He looked at Terens.

Terens said, "I witness. Girls awaken early, don't they?"

Palino, tapping away, said, "Mother, Sigrid, also of Upland Holding."

At which Lewin leaned forward. "Cleared by this court," he said. I was relieved to hear that. Mother is clever. She hadn't let them know she knew.

Palino said, "And your father is?"

"Timas, Donal, and Yan," I said. I had to bite the inside of my cheek not to laugh at how annoyed he was by that.

"Great Tew, girl!" he said. "A person can't have three fathers!"

"Hold it, Palino," said Lewin. "You're up against local customs here. Men outnumber women three to one on Home Eight."

"In Home Eight law a woman's child is the child of all her husbands equally," Renick put in. "No more anomalous than the status of the Ahrings on Seven, really."

"Then tell me how I rephrase my question," Palino said waspishly, "in the light of the primitive customs on Home Eight."

I said, "There's no such place as Home Eight. This world is called Sveridge." Primitive indeed!

Palino gave me a pale glare. I gave him one back. Lewin cut in, smooth and humorous. "You're up against primitive Dragonate customs here, Siglin. We refer to all the worlds by numbers, from Albion, Home One, to Yurov, Home Ten, and the worlds of the Outer Manifold are Cath One, Two, Three, and Four to us. Have you really no idea which of your mother's husbands is actually your father?"

After that they all began asking me. Being heg is inherited, and I knew they were trying to find out if any of my fathers was heg, too. At length even Alectis joined in, clearing his throat and going very red because he was only a cadet. "I know we're not supposed to know," he said, "but I bet you've tried to guess. I did. I found out in the end."

That told me he was Sveridge, too. And he suddenly wasn't a genius in the Camerati anymore, but just a boy. "Then I bet you wished you hadn't!" I said. "My friend Inga at Hillfoot found out, and hers turned out to be the one she's always hated."

"Well," said Alectis, redder still. "Er, it wasn't the one I'd hoped—"

"That's why I've never asked," I said. And that was true. I'd always hoped it was Timas till now. Donal is so moral, and Yan is fun, but he's under Donal's thumb even more than he's under Mother's. But I didn't want my dear old Timas in trouble.

"Well, a cell test should settle it," Lewin said. "Memo for that, Palino. Terens, remind me to ask how the regular Dragonate usually deals with it. Now, Siglin, this charge was laid against you by a man known as Orm the Worm Warden. Do you know this man?"

"Don't I just!" I said. "He's been coming here and looking through our windows and giggling ever since I can remember! He lives on the Worm Reserve in a shack. Mother says he's a bit wrong in the head, but no one's locked him up because he's so good at managing dragons."

There! I thought. That'll show them you can't trust a word Orm says! But they just nodded. Terens murmured to Alectis, "Sveridge worm, *Draco draco*, was adopted as the symbol of the Dragonate—"

"We *have* all heard of dragons," Palino said to him nastily.

Lewin cut in again. I suppose it was his job as presiding Updriten. "Siglin, Orm, in his deposition, refers to an incident in the Worm Reserve last Friday. We want you to tell us what happened then, if anything."

Grim's teeth! I thought. I'd hoped they'd just ask me questions. You can nearly always get around questions without lying. And I'd no idea what Orm had said. "I don't usually go to the Dragon Reserve," I said, "because of being Mother's heir. When I was born, the Fortune Teller said the dragons would take me." I saw Renick and Palino exchange looks of contempt at our primitive customs. But Mother had in a good Teller, and I believe it enough to keep away from the Reserve.

"So why did you go last Friday?" said Lewin.

"Neal dared me to," I said. I couldn't say anything else with a lie detector in my hands. Neal gets on with Orm, and he goes to the Reserve a lot. Up to Friday he thought I was being silly refusing to go. But the real trouble was that Neal had been there all along, riding Barra beside me on Nellie, and now Lewin had made me mention Neal, I couldn't think how to pretend he hadn't been there. "I rode up behind Wormhill," I said, "and then over the Saddle until we could see the sea. That means you're in the Reserve."

"Isn't the Reserve fenced off at all?" Renick asked disapprovingly.

"No," I said. "Worms—dragons—can fly, so what's the point? They stay in because the shepherds bombard them if they don't, and we all give them so many sheep every month." And Orm makes them stay in, bad cess to him! "Anyway," I said, "I was riding down a kyle—that's what we call those narrow stony valleys—when my horse reared and threw me. Next thing I knew—"

"Question," said Palino. "Where was your brother at this point?"

He *would* spot that! I thought. "Some way behind," I said. Six feet, in fact. Barra is used to dragons and just stood stock-still. "This dragon shuffled head down with its great snout across the kyle," I said. "I sat on the ground with its great amused eye staring at me and listening to Nellie clattering away up the kyle. It was a youngish one, sort of brown-green, which is why I hadn't seen it. They can keep awfully still when they want to. And I said a rude word to it.

" 'That's no way to speak to a dragon!' Orm said. He was sitting on a rock on the other side of the kyle, quite close, laughing at me." I wondered whether to fill the gap in my story where Neal was by telling them that Orm always used to be my idea of Jack Frost when I was little. He used to call at Uplands for milk then, to feed dragon fledglings on, but he was so rude to Mother that he goes to Inga's place now. Orm is long and skinny and brown, with a great white bush of hair and beard, and he smells rather. But they must have smelled him in Holmstad, so I said, "I was scared because the dragon was so near I could feel the heat off it. And then Orm said, 'You have to speak politely to this dragon. He's my particular friend. You give me a nice kiss, and he'll let you go.' "

I think Lewin murmured something like, "Ah, I thought it might be that!" but it may just have been in his mind. I don't know because I was in real trouble then, trying to pick my way through without mentioning Neal. The little box got so wet it nearly slipped out of my hand. I said, "Every time I tried to get up, Orm beckoned, and the dragon pushed me down with its snout with a gamesome look in its eye. And Orm cackled with laughter. They were both really having fun." This was true, but the dragon also pushed between me and Neal and mantled its wings when Neal tried to help. And Neal said some pretty awful things to Orm. Orm giggled and insulted Neal back. He called Neal a booby who couldn't stand up for himself against women.

"Then," I said, "then Orm said I was the image of Mother at the same age—which isn't true: I'm bigger all over—and he said, 'Come on, kiss and be friends!' Then he skipped down from his rock and took hold of my arm—"

I had to stop and swallow there. The really awful thing was that as soon as Orm had hold of me, I got a strong picture from his mind: Orm kissing a pretty lady smaller than me, with another dragon, an older, blacker one, looking on from the background. And I recognized the lady as Mother, and I was absolutely disgusted.

"So I hit Orm and got up and ran away," I said. "And Orm shouted to me all the time I was running up the kyle and catching Nellie, but I took no notice."

"Question," said Renick. "What action did the dragon take?"

"They—they always chase you if you run, I'd heard," Alectis said shyly.

"And this one appears to have been trained to Orm's command," Palino said.

"It didn't chase me," I said. "It stayed with Orm." The reason was that neither of them could move. I still don't know what I did—I had a picture of myself leaning back inside my own head and swinging mighty blows, the way you do with a pickax—and Neal says the dragon went over like a cartload of potatoes and Orm fell flat on his back. But Orm could speak, and he screamed after us that I'd killed the worm and I'd pay for it. But I was screaming, too, at Neal, to keep away from me because I was heg. That was the thing that horrified me most. Before that I'd tried not to think I was. After all, for all I knew, everyone can read minds and get a book from the bookcase without getting up from his chair. And Neal told me to pull myself together and think what we were going to tell Mother. We decided to say that we'd met a dragon in the Reserve and I'd killed it and found out I was heg. I made Neal promise not to mention Orm. I couldn't bear even to think of Orm. And Mother was wonderfully understanding, and I really didn't realize that I'd put her in danger as well as Neal.

Lewin looked down at the recorder. "Dragons are a preserved species," he said. "Orm claims that you caused grievous bodily harm to a dragon in his care. What have you to say to that?"

"How could I?" I said. Oh, I was scared. "It was nearly as big as a house."

Renick was on to that at once. "Query," he said. "Prevarication?"

"Obviously," said Palino, clicking away at his block.

"We haven't looked at that dragon yet," Terens said.

"We'll do that on our way back," Lewin said, sighing rather. "Siglin, I regret to say there is enough mismatch between your account and Orm's, and enough odd activity on that brain measure you hold in your hand, to warrant my taking you to Holmstad Command Center for further examination. Be good enough to go with Terens and Alectis to the van, and wait there while we complete our inquiries here."

I stood up. Everything seemed to drain out of me. I could lam them like I lammed that dragon, I thought. But Holmstad would only send a troop out to see why they hadn't come back. And I put my oldest dress on for nothing! I thought as I walked down the hallway with Terens and Alectis. The doors were all closed. Everyone had guessed. The van smelled of clean plastic, and it was very warm and light because the roof was one big window. I sat between Terens and Alectis on the backseat. They pulled straps around us all—safety straps, but they made me feel a true prisoner.

After a while Terens said, "You could sue Orm if the evidence doesn't hold up, you know." I think he was trying to be kind, but I couldn't answer.

After another while Alectis said, "With respect, Driten, I

think suspects should be told the truth about the so-called lie detector."

"Alectis, I didn't hear you say that," Terens said. He pretended to look out of the window, but he must have known I knew he had deliberately thought *lie detector* at me as he passed me the thing. They're told to. Dragonate think of everything. I sat and thought I'd never hated anything so much as I hated our kind, self-sacrificing Dragonate, and I tried to take a last look at the stony yard, tipped sideways on the hill, with our square stone house at the top of it. But it wouldn't register somehow.

Then the front door opened, and the other three came out, bringing Neal with them. Behind them the hall was full of our people, with Mother in front, just staring. I just stared, too, while Palino opened the van door and shoved Neal into the seat beside me. "Your brother has admitted being present at the incident," he said as he strapped himself in beside Neal. I could tell he was pleased.

By this time Lewin and Renick had strapped themselves into the front seat. Lewin drove away without a word. Neal looked back at the house. I couldn't. "Neal—?" I whispered.

"Just like you said," Neal said, loudly and defiantly. "Behaving as if they own the Ten Worlds. I wouldn't join now if they begged me to!" Why did I have to go and say that to him? "Why did *you* join?" Neal said rudely to Alectis.

"Six brothers," Alectis said, staring ahead.

The other four all started talking at once. Lewin asked Renick the quickest way to the Reserve by road, and Renick said it was down through Wormstow. "I hope the dragons eat you!" Neal said. This was while Palino was leaning across us to say to Terens, "Where's our next inspection after this hole?" And Terens said, "We go straight on to Arkloren on Nine. Alectis will get to see some other parts of the Manifold shortly." Behaving as if we didn't exist. Neal shrugged and shut up.

The Dragonate van was much smoother and faster than a farm van. We barely bounced over the stony track that loops down to Hillfoot, and it seemed no time before we were speeding down the better road, with the rounded yellowish Upland Hills peeling past on either side. I love my hills, covered with yellow ling that only grows here on Sveridge, and the soft light of the sun through our white and gray clouds. Renick, still making conversation, said he was surprised to find the hills so old and worn down. "I thought Eight was a close parallel with Seven!" he said.

Lewin answered in a boring voice, "I wouldn't know. I haven't seen Seven since I was a cadet."

"Oh, the mountains are much higher and greener there," Renick said. "I was posted in Camberia for years. Lovely spot."

Lewin just grunted. Quite a wave of homesickness filled the van. I could feel Renick thinking of Seven and Alectis not wanting to go to Nine. Terens was remembering boating on Romaine when he was Neal's age. Lewin was thinking of Seven, in spite of the grunt. We were coming over Jiot Fell already then, with the Giant Stones standing on top of the world against the sky. A few more turns in the road would bring us out above Wormstow where Neal and I went—used to go—to school. What about me? I was thinking. I'm homesick for life. And Neal. Poor Mother.

Then the air suddenly filled with noise, like the most gigantic sheet being torn.

Lewin said, "What the—?" and we all stared upward. A great silvery shape screamed overhead. And another of a fatter shape, more blue than silver, screamed after it, both of them only just inside the clouds. Alectis put up an astonished pointing arm. "Thraller! The one behind's a Slaver!"

"What's it doing *here?*" said Terens. "Someone must have slipped up."

"Ours was a stratoship!" said Palino. "What's going on?"

A huge ball of fire rolled into being on the horizon, above the

Giant Stones. I felt Lewin slam on the brakes. "We got him!" one of them cried out.

"The Slaver got ours," Lewin said. The brakes were still yelling like a she-worm when the blast hit.

I lose the next bit. I start remembering again a few seconds later, sitting up straight with a bruised lip, finding the van around sideways a long way on down the road. In front of me Renick's straps had broken. He was lying kind of folded against the windscreen. I saw Lewin pull himself upright and pull at Renick. And stop pulling quickly. My ears had gone deaf, because I could only hear Lewin as if he were very far off. "—hurt in the back?"

Palino looked along the four of us and shouted, "Fine! Is Renick—?"

"Dead," Lewin shouted back. "Neck broken." He was jiggling furiously at buttons in the controls. My ears started to work again, and I heard him say, "Holmstad's not answering. Nor's Ranefell. I'm going back to Holmstad. Fast."

We set off again with a roar. The van seemed to have lost its silencer, and it rattled all over, but it went. And how it went. We must have done nearly a hundred down Jiot, squealing on the bends. In barely minutes we could see Wormstow spread out below, old gray houses and new white ones, and all those imported trees that make the town so pretty. The clouds over the houses seemed to darken and go dense.

"Uh-oh!" said Terens.

The van jolted to another yelling stop. It was not the clouds. Something big and dark was coming down through the clouds, slowly descending over Wormstow. Something enormous. "What *is* that?" Neal and Alectis said together.

"Hedgehog," said Terens.

"A slaveship," Palino explained, sort of mincing the word out to make it mean more. "Are—are we out of range here?"

"I most thoroughly hope so," Lewin said. "There's not much we can do with hand weapons."

We sat and stared as the thing came down. The lower it got, the more Renick's bent-up shape was in my way. I kept wishing Lewin would do something about him, but nobody seemed to be able to think of anything but that huge descending ship. I saw why they call them hedgehogs. It was rounded above and flat beneath, with bits and pieces sticking out all over like bristles. Hideous somehow. And it came and hung squatting over the roofs of the houses below. There it let out a ramp like a long black tongue, right down into the Market Square. Then another into High Street, between the rows of trees, breaking a tree as it passed.

As soon as the ramps touched ground, Lewin started the van and drove down toward Wormstow.

"No, stop!" I said, even though I knew he couldn't. The compulsion those Slavers put out is really strong. Some of it shouts inside your head, like your own conscience through an amplifier, and some of it is gentle and creeping and insidious, like Mother telling you gently to come along now and be sensible. I found I was thinking, Oh, well, I'm sure Lewin's right. Tears rolled down Alectis's face, and Neal was sniffing. We had to go to the ship, which was now hanging a little above us. I could see people hurrying out of houses and racing to crowd up the ramp in the Market Square. People I knew. So it must be all right, I thought. The van was having to weave past loose horses that people had been riding or driving. That was how I got a glimpse of the other ramp, through trees and the legs of a horse. Soldiers were pouring down it, running like a muddy river, in waves. Each wave had a little group of kings, walking behind it, directing the soldiers. They had shining crowns and shining Vs on their chests and walked mighty, like gods.

That brought me to my senses. "Lewin," I said, "those are

Thrallers, and you're *not* to do what they say, do you hear?"
Lewin just drove around a driverless cart, toward the Market
Square. He was going to be driving up that ramp in a second. I
was so frightened then that I lammed Lewin—not like I lammed
the dragon, but in a different way. Again it's hard to describe,
except that this time I was giving orders. Lewin was to obey *me*,
not the Thrallers, and my orders were to drive away *at once*.
When nothing seemed to happen, I got so scared that I seemed
to be filling the whole van with my orders.

"Thank you," Lewin said in a croaking sort of voice. He
jerked the van around into Worm Parade and roared down it,
away from the ship and the terrible ramps. The swerve sent the
van door open with a slam, and to my relief, the body of poor
Renick tumbled out into the road.

But everyone else screamed out, "No! What are you doing?"
and clutched their heads. The compulsion was far, far worse if
you disobeyed. I felt as if layers of my brain were being peeled
off with hot pincers. Neal was crying, like Alectis. Terens was
moaning. It hurt so much that I filled the van frantically with
more and more orders. Lewin made grinding sounds deep in his
throat and kept on driving away, with the door flapping and
banging.

Palino took his straps undone and yelled, "You're going the
wrong way, you damn cariarder!" I couldn't stop him at all. He
started to climb into the front seat to take the controls away
from Lewin. Alectis and Neal both rose up, too, and shoved him
off Lewin. So Palino gave that up and scrambled for the open
flapping door instead. Nobody could do a thing. He just
jumped out and went rolling in the road. I didn't see what he
did then, because I was too busy giving orders, but Neal says he
simply scrambled up and staggered back toward the ship and the
ramp.

We drove for another horrible half mile, and then we must

have got out of range. Everything suddenly went easy. It was like when somebody lets go the other end of a rope you're both pulling, and you go over backward. Wham. And I felt too dim and stunned to move.

"Thank the gods!" I heard Terens more or less howl.

"It's Siglin you should be thanking," Lewin said. "Alectis, climb over to the front and shut that door. Then try and raise Holmstad again."

Neal said the door was too battered to shut. Alectis had to hold it with one hand while he worked the broadcaster with the other. I heard him saying that Holmstad still didn't answer through the roaring and rattling the van made when Lewin put on speed up the long, looping gradient of Wormjiot. We had nearly got up to the Saddle when Terens said, "It's going! Aren't they quick?" I looked back, still feeling dim and horrible, in time to see the squatting hedgehog rise up inside the clouds again.

"Now you can thank the gods," Lewin said. "They didn't think we were worth chasing. Try medium wave, Alectis." There is an outcrop of ragged rock near the head of Wormjiot. Lewin drove off the road and stopped behind it while Alectis fiddled with knobs.

Instead of getting dance music and cookery hints, Alectis got a voice that fizzed and crackled. "This is Dragonate Fanejiot, Sveridge South, with an emergency message for all Dragonate units still in action. You are required to make your way to Fane-jiot and report there soonest." It said that about seven times. Then it said, "We can now confirm earlier reports that Home Nine is in Slaver hands. Here is a list of bases on Home Eight that have been taken by Slavers." It was a long list. Holmstad came quite early on it, and Ranefell about ten names after that.

Lewin reached across and turned it off. "Did someone say we slipped up?" he said. "That was an understatement."

"Fanejiot is two thousand flaming miles from here!" Terens

said. "With an ocean and who knows how many Slavers in between!"

"Well put," said Lewin. "Did Palino's memo block go to the Slavers with him?"

It was lying on the backseat beside Neal. Neal tried to pretend it wasn't, but Alectis turned around and grabbed it as Neal tried to shove it on the floor. I was lying back in my straps, feeling gray and thinking, We could get away now. I'd better lam them all again. But all I did was lie there and watch Neal and Alectis having an angry tug-of-war. Then watch Lewin turn around and pluck the block away from the pair of them.

"Don't be a fool," he said to Neal. "I've already erased the recorder. And if I hadn't had Renick and Palino breathing righteously down our necks, I'd never have recorded anything. It goes against the grain to take in children."

Lewin pressed the *erase* on the memo block, and it gave out a satisfied sort of gobble. Neither of the other two said anything, but I could feel Alectis thinking how much he had always hated Palino. Terens was looking down at Wormstow through a fieldglass and trying not to remember a boy in Cadets with him who had turned heg and given himself up. I felt I wanted to say thank you. But I was too shy to do anything but sit up and look at Wormstow, too, between the jags of the rock. Even without a fieldglass, I could see the place throbbing like a broken anthill with all the Slaver troops.

"Getting ready to move out and mop up the countryside," Terens said.

"Yes, and that's where most people live," Lewin said. "Farms and holdings in the hills. What's the quickest way to the Dragon Reserve?"

"There's a track on the right around the next bend," said Neal. "Why?"

"Because it's the safest place I can think of," Lewin said.

Neal and I looked at one another. You didn't need to be heg

to tell that Neal was thinking, just as I was, that this was a bit much. They were supposed to help all those people in the holdings. Instead, they thought of the safest place and ran there! So neither of us said that the trade was only a bridle path, and we didn't try to warn them not to take the van into the Reserve. We just sat there while Lewin drove it uphill and then lumping and bumping and rattling up the path. The path gave out in the marshy patch below the Saddle, but Lewin kept grinding and roaring on, throwing up peat in squirts, until we tipped downhill again and bounced down a yellow fellside. We were in the Reserve by then. The ling was growing in lurid green patches, black at the roots where dragons had burned it in the mating season. They fight a lot then.

We got some way into the Reserve. The van gave out clanging sounds and smelled bad, but Lewin kept it going by driving on the most level parts. We were in a wide stony scoop, with yellow hills all around, when the smell got worse and the van just stopped. Alectis let go of the door. "Worms—dragons," he said, "don't like machines, I've heard."

"Now he tells us!" said Terens, and we all got out. We all looked as if we had been in an accident. I mean, I know we had in a way, but we looked worse than I'd expected: sort of ragged and pale and shivery. Lewin turned his foot on a stone, which made him clutch his chest and swear. Neither of the other two even asked if he was all right. That is the Dragonate way. They just set out walking. Neal and I went with them, thinking of the best place to dodge off up a kyle, so that we could run home and try and warn Mother about the Slavers.

"Where that bog turns into a stream—I'll say when," Neal was whispering, when a dragon came over the hill into the valley and made straight for us.

"Stand still!" said Alectis. Lewin and Terens each had a gun in his hand without seeming to have moved. Alectis didn't, and he was white.

"They only eat moving prey," Neal said, because he was sorry for him. "Make sure not to panic and run, and you're fine."

I was sorry for Alectis, too, so I added, "It's probably only after the van. They love metal."

Lewin crumpled his face at me and said "Ah!" for some reason.

The dragon came quite slowly, helping itself with its spread wings and hanging its head rather. It was a bad color, sort of creamy through the brown-green. I thought it might be one of the sick ones that turn man-eater, and I tried to brace myself and stop feeling so tired and shaky so that I could lam it. But Neal said, "That's Orm's dragon! You didn't kill it after all!"

It *was* Orm's dragon. By this time it was near enough for me to see the heat off it quivering in the air, and I recognized the gamesome, shrewd look in its eye. But since it had every reason to hate me, that didn't make me feel much better. It came straight for me, too. We all stood like statues. And it came right up to me and bent its neck and laid its huge brown head on the ling in front of my feet, where it puffed out a sigh that made Lewin cough and gasp another swearword.

It had felt me coming, the dragon said, and it was here to say sorry. It hadn't meant to upset me. It had thought it was a game.

That made me feel terrible. "I'm sorry, too," I said. "I lost my head. I didn't mean to hurt you. That was Orm's fault."

Orm was only playing, too, the dragon said. Orm called him Huffle, and I could, too, if I liked. Was he forgiven? He was ashamed.

"Of course I forgive you, Huffle," I said. "Do you forgive me?"

Yes. Huffle lifted his head up and went a proper color at once. Dragons are like people that way.

"Ask him to fetch Orm here," Lewin said urgently.

I didn't want to see Orm, and Lewin was a coward. "Ask him yourself," I said. "He understands."

"Yes, but I don't think he'd do it for me," Lewin said.

"Then, will you fetch Orm for Lewin?" I asked Huffle.

He gave me a cheeky look. Maybe. Presently. He sauntered away past Terens, who moved his head back from Huffle's rattling right wing, looking as if he thought his last hour had come, and went to have a look at the van. He put out a great clawed foot, in a thoughtful sort of way, and tore the loose door off it. Then he tucked the door under his right front foreleg and departed, deliberately slowly, on three legs, helping himself with his wings, so that rocks rattled and flapped all along the valley.

Alectis sat down rather suddenly. But Lewin made him leap up again and help Terens get the broadcaster out of the van before any more dragons found it. They never did get it out. They were still working and waggling at it to get it loose, and Lewin was standing over Neal and me, so that we couldn't sneak off, when we heard that humming kind of whistle that you get from a dragon in flight. We whirled around. This dragon was a big black one, coasting low over the hill opposite and gliding down the valley. They don't often fly high. It came to ground with that grinding of stones and leathery slap of wings closing that always tells you a dragon is landing. It arched its black neck and looked at us disdainfully.

Orm was sitting on its back looking equally disdainful. It was one of those times when Orm looks grave and grand. He sat very upright, with his hair and beard combed straight by the wind of flying, and his big pale eyes hardly looked mad at all. Neal was the only one of us he deigned to notice. "Good afternoon, Neal Sigridsson," he said. "You keep bad company. Dragonate are not human."

Neal was very angry with Orm. He put my heart in my mouth by saying, quite calmly, "Then in that case, I'm the only human here." With that dragon standing glaring! I've been brought up to despise boys, but I think that is a mistake.

To my relief, Orm just grinned. "That's the way, boy," he said. "Not a booby after all, are you?"

Then Lewin took my breath away by going right up to the dragon. He had his gun, of course, but that wouldn't have been much use against a dragon. He went so near that the dragon had to turn its head out of his way. "We've dropped the charges," he said. "And you should never have brought them."

Orm looked down at him. "You," he said, "know a thing or two."

"I know dragons don't willingly attack humans," Lewin said. "I always read up on a case before I hear it." At this, Orm put on his crazy look and made his mad cackle. "Stop that!" said Lewin. "The Slavers have invaded. Wormstow's full of Slaver troops, and we need your help. I want to get everyone from the outlying farms into the Reserve and persuade the dragons to protect them. Can you help us do that?"

That took my breath away again, and Neal's, too. We did a quick goggle at one another. Perhaps the Dragonate was the way it was supposed to be after all!

Orm said, "Then we'd better get busy," and slid down from the dragon. He still towered over Lewin. Orm is huge. As soon as he was down, the black dragon lumbered across to the van and started taking it to bits. That brought other dragons coasting, whistling in from all sides of the valley, to crunch to earth and hurry to the van, too. In seconds it was surrounded by black and green-brown shapes the size of hay barns. And Orm talked, at the top of his voice, through the sound of metal tearing, and big claws screaming on iron, and wings clapping, and angry grunts when two dragons happened to get hold of the same piece of van. Orm always talks a lot. But this time he was being particularly garrulous, to give the dragons time to lumber away with their pieces of van, hide them, and come back. "They won't even do what Orm says until they've got their metal," I whispered to Terens, who got rather impatient with Orm.

Orm said the best place to put people was the high valley at the center of the Reserve. "There's an old she-drake with a litter just hatched," he said. "No one will get past her when she's feared for her young. I'll speak to her. But the rest are to promise me she's not disturbed." As for telling everyone at the farms where to come, Orm said the dragons could do that, provided Lewin could think of a way of sending a message by them. "You see, most folk can't hear a dragon when it speaks," he said. "And some who can hear"—with a nasty look at me—"speak back to wound." He was still very angry with me. I kept on the other side of Terens and Alectis when the dragons all came swooping back.

Terens set the memo block to *repeat* and tapped out an official message from Lewin. Then he tore off page after page with the same thing on it. Orm handed each page to a dragon, saying things like "Take this to the fat cow up at Hillfoot." Or "Drop this on young vinegar lady at Crowtop—hard." Or "This is for Dopey at High Jiot, but don't give it her; give it to her youngest husband or they'll never get moving."

Some of the things he said made me laugh a lot. But it was only when Alectis asked what was so funny and Neal kicked my ankle that I realized I was the only one who could hear the things Orm said. Each dragon, as it got its page, ran down the valley and took off, showering us with stones from the jump it gave to get higher in the air than usual. Their wings boom when they fly high. Orm took off on the black dragon last of all, saying he would go and warn the she-drake.

Lewin crumpled his face ruefully at the few bits of van remaining, and we set off to walk to the valley ourselves. It was a long way. Over ling slopes and up among boulders in the kyles we trudged, looking up nervously every so often when fat bluish Slaver fliers screamed through the clouds overhead. After a while our dragons began booming overhead, too, seaward to roost. Terens counted them and said every one we had sent seemed to have come back now. He said he wished he had wings. It was sunset by the time we reached the valley. By that time Lewin was bent over, holding his chest and swearing every other step. But everyone was still pretending, in that stupid Dragonate way, that he was all right. We came up on the cliffs, where the kyle winds down to the she-drake's valley, and there was the sunset lighting the sea and the towers of rock out there, and the waves crashing around the rocks, where the young dragons were flying to roost, and Lewin actually pretended to admire the view. "I knew a place like this on Seven," he said. "Except there were trees instead of dragons. I can't get used to the way Eight doesn't have trees."

He was going to sit down to rest, I think, but Orm came up the kyle just then. Huffle was hulking behind him. "So you got here at last!" Orm said in his rudest way.

"We have," said Lewin. "Now would you mind telling me what you were playing at bringing those charges against Siglin?"

"You should be glad I did. You'd all be in a slaveship now if I hadn't," Orm said.

"But you weren't to know that, were you?" Terens said.

"Not to speak of risking being charged yourself," added Lewin.

Orm leaned on his hand against Huffle, as you might against a wall. "She half killed this dragon!" he said. "That's why! All I did was ask her for a kiss, and she screams and lays into poor Huffle. My own daughter, and she tries to kill a dragon! And I thought, Right, my lady, then you're no daughter of mine anymore! And I flew Huffle's mother straight into Holmstad and laid charges. I was that angry! My own father tended dragons, and his mother before him. And my daughter tried to kill one! You wonder I was angry?"

"Nobody *told* me!" I said. I had that draining-away feeling again.

I was quite glad when Terens took hold of my elbow and said something like "Steady, steady!"

"Are you telling the truth?" Neal said.

"I'm sure he is," Lewin said. "Your sister has his eyes."

"Ask Timas," said Orm. "He married your mother the year after I did. He can take being bossed about. I can't. I went back to my dragons. But I suppose there's a record of that?" he said challengingly to Lewin.

"And the divorce," said Lewin. "Terens looked it up for me. But I expect the Slavers have destroyed it by now."

"And she never told you?" Orm said to me. He wagged his shaggy eyebrows at me almost forgivingly. "I'll have a bone to pick with her over that," he said.

Mother arrived just as we'd all got down into the valley. She looked very indomitable, as she always does on horseback, and all our people were with her, down to both our shepherds. They had carts of clothes and blankets and food. Mother knew the valley as well as Orm did. She used to meet Orm there when she was a girl. She set out for the Reserve as soon as she heard the broadcast about the invasion, and the dragon we sent her met them on the way. That's Mother for you. The rest of the neighbors didn't get there for some hours after that.

I didn't think Mother's face—or Timas's—could hold such a mixture of feelings as they did when they saw Neal and me and the Dragonate men all with Orm. When Orm saw Mother, he folded his arms and grinned. Huffle rested his huge chin on Orm's shoulder, looking interested.

"Here she comes," Orm said to Huffle. "Oh, I do love a good quarrel!"

They had one. It was one of the loudest I'd ever heard. Terens took Neal and me away to help look after Lewin. He turned out to have broken some ribs when the blast hit the van, but he wouldn't let anyone look even until I ordered him to. After that Neal, Alectis, and I sat under our hay cart and talked, mostly about the irony of Fate. You see, Neal has always secretly wished Fate had given him Orm as a father, and I'm the one that's got Orm. Neal's father is Timas. Alectis says he can see the likeness. We'd both gladly swap. Then Alectis confessed that he'd been hating the Dragonate so much that he was thinking of running away, which is a serious crime. But now the Slavers have come, and there doesn't seem to be much of a Dragonate anymore, he feels quite different. He admires Lewin.

Lewin consented to rest while Terens and Mother organized everyone into a makeshift camp in the valley, but he was up and about again the next day, because he said the Slavers were bound to come the day after, when they found the holdings were deserted. The big black she-drake sat in her cave at the head of the kyle, with her infants between her forefeet, watching groups of people rushing around to do what Lewin said, and didn't seem to mind at all. Huffle said she'd been bored and bad-tempered up to then. We made life interesting. Actually that she-drake reminds me of Mother. Both of them made me give them a faithful report of the battle.

I don't think the Slavers knew about the dragons. They just knew that there was a concentration of people in here, and they came straight across the Reserve to get us. As soon as the dragons told Orm they were coming, Lewin had us all out hiding in the hills in their path, except for Mother and Timas and Inga's mother and a few more who had shotguns. They had to stay and guard the little kids in the camp. The rest of us had any weapons we could find. Neal and Alectis had bows and arrows. Inga had her airgun. Donal and most of the farmers had scythes. The shepherds all had their slingshots. I was in the front with Lewin, because I was supposed to stop the effect of the Slavers' collars. Orm was there, too, although nobody had ever admitted in so many words that Orm might be heg. All Orm did was to ask the dragons to keep back because we didn't want *them* enslaved by those collars.

And there they came, a huddle of sheeplike troops, and then another huddle, each one being driven by a cluster of kingly Slavers, with crowns and winking V-shaped collars And there again we all got that horrible guilty compulsion to come and give ourselves up. But I don't think those collars have any effect on dragons. Half of us were standing up to walk into the Slavers' arms, and I was ordering them as hard as I could not to, when the dragons smelled those golden crowns and collars: there was no holding them. They just whirred down over our heads and took those Slavers to pieces for the metal. Lewin said, "Ah!" and crumpled his face in a grin like a fiend's. He'd thought the dragons might do that. I think he may really be a genius, like they say Camerati are. But I was so sick at that, and then again at the sight of nice people like Alectis and Yan killing the sheeplike troops, that I'm not going to talk about it anymore. Terens says I'm not to go when the Slavers come next. Apparently I broadcast the way I was feeling, just as the Slavers do, and even the dragons felt queasy. The she-drake snorted at that. Mother says, "Nonsense. Take travel pills and behave as my daughter should."

Anyway, we have found out how to beat the Slavers. We have no idea what is going on in the other of the Ten Worlds, or even in the rest of Sveridge, but there are fifty more Worm Reserves around the world, and Lewin says there must be stray Dragonate units, too, who might think of using dragons against Slavers. We want to move out and take over some of the farms again soon. The dragons are having far too much fun with the sheep. They keep flying over with woolly bundles dangling from their claws, watched by a gloomy crowd of everyone's shepherds. "Green dot," the shepherds say. "The brutes are raiding Hightop now." They are very annoyed with Orm because Orm just gives his mad cackle and lets the dragons go on.

Orm isn't mad at all. He's afraid of people knowing he's heg; he still won't admit he is. I think that's why he left Mother, and Mother doesn't admit she was ever married to him. Not that Mother minds. I get the feeling she and Orm understand one another rather well. But Mother married Donal, you see, after Timas. Donal, and Yan, too, have both told me that the fact that I'm heg makes no difference to them, but you should see the way they both look at me! I'm not fooled. I don't blame Orm for being scared stiff Donal would find out he was heg. But I'm not sure I shall ever like Orm, all the same.

I am putting all this down on what is left of Palino's memo block. Lewin wanted me to, in case there is still some history yet to come. He has made his official version on the recorder. I'm leaning the block on Huffle's forefoot. Huffle is my friend now. Leaning on a dragon is the best way to keep warm on a chilly evening like this, when you're forced to camp out in the Reserve. Huffle is letting Lewin lean on him, too, beyond Neal, because Lewin's ribs still pain him. There is a lot of leaning space along the side of a dragon. Orm has just stepped across Huffle's tail, into the light, chortling and rubbing his hands in his most irritating way.

"Your mother's on the warpath," he says. "Oh, I do love a good quarrel!"

And here comes Mother, ominously upright, and with her arms folded. It's not Orm she wants. It's Lewin. "Listen, you," she says. "What the dickens is the Dragonate thinking of, beheading hegs all these years? They can't help what they are. And they're the only people who can stand up to the Thrallers."

Orm is cheated of his quarrel. Lewin looked up, crumpled into the most friendly smile. "I do so agree with you," he said. "I've just said so in my report. And I'd have got your daughter off somehow, you know."

Orm is cackling like the she-drake's young ones. Mother's mouth is open, and I really think that for once in her life she has no idea what to say.

WHAT THE CAT
TOLD ME

I am a cat. I am a cat like anything. Keep stroking me. I came in here because I knew you were good at stroking. But put your knees together so I can sit properly, front paws under. That's better. Now keep stroking, don't forget to rub my ears, and I will purr and tell.

I am going to tell you how I came to be so very old. When I was a kitten, humans dressed differently, and they had great stamping horses to pull their cars and buses. The Old Man in the house where I lived used to light a hissing gas on the wall when it got dark. He wore a long black coat. The Boy who was nice to me wore shabby breeches that only came to his knees, and he mostly went without shoes, just like me. We slept in a cupboard under the stairs, Boy and I. We kept one another warm. We kept one another fed, too, later on. The Old Man did not like cats or boys. He only kept us because we were useful.

I was more useful than Boy. I had to sit in a five-pointed star. The Boy would help Old Man mix things that smoked and made me sneeze. I had to sneeze three times. After that things happened. Sometimes big purple cloud things came and sat beside me in the star. Fur stood up on me, and I spat, but the things only went away when Old Man hit the star with his stick and told them, *"Begone!"* in a loud voice. At other times the things that came were small, real things you could hit with your paw: boxes, or strings of shiny stones no one could eat, or bright rings that fell *tink* beside me out of nowhere. I did not mind those things. The things I really hated were the third kind.

Those came inside me and used my mouth to speak. They were nasty things with hateful thoughts, and they made *me* hateful. And my mouth does not like to speak. It ached afterward, and my tongue and throat were so sore that I could not wash the hatefulness off me for hours.

I so hated those inside-speaking things that I used to run away and hide when I saw Old Man drawing the star on the cellar floor. I am good at hiding. Sometimes it took Boy half the day to find me. Then Old Man would shout and curse and hit Boy and call him a fool. Boy cried at night in the cupboard afterward. I did not like that, so after a while I scratched Old Man instead. I knew none of it was Boy's fault. Boy made Old Man give me nice things to eat after I had sat in the star. He said it was the only way to get me to sit there.

Boy was clever, you see. Old Man thought he was a fool, but Boy told me—at night in the cupboard—that he only pretended to be stupid. Boy was an orphan like me. Old Man had bought him for a shilling from a baby farmer ages before I was even a kitten, because his hair was orange, like the ginger patches on me, and that is supposed to be a good color for magic. Old Man paid a whole farthing for me, for much the same reason, because I am brindled. And Boy had been with Old Man ever since, learning things. It was not only magic that Boy learned. Old Man was away quite a lot when Boy was small. Boy used to read Old Man's books in the room upstairs, and the newspapers, and anything else he could find. He told me he wanted to learn magic in order to escape from Old Man, and he learned the other things so that he could manage in the wide world when he did escape; but he had been a prisoner in the house for years now, and although he knew a great deal, he still could not break the spell Old Man had put on him to keep him inside the house. "And I really hate him," Boy said to me, "because of the cat before you. I want to stop him doing any more magic before I leave."

And I said—

What was that? How could Boy and I talk together? Do you think I am a stupid cat, or something? I am nearly as clever as Boy. How do you think I am telling you all this? Let me roll over. My stomach needs rubbing. Oh, you rub well! I really like you. Well— No, let me sit up again now. I think the talking must be something to do with those inside-speaking things. When I was a kitten, I could understand what people said, of course, but I couldn't do it back, not at first, until I had been lived in and been spoken through by quite a lot of Things. Boy thought they stretched my mind. And I was clever to start with, not like the cat before me.

Old Man killed the cat before me somehow. Boy would not tell me how. It was a stupid cat, he said, but he loved it. After he told me that, I would not go near Boy for a whole day. It was not just that I was nervous about being killed, too. How *could* he love any cat that wasn't *me*? Boy caught me a pigeon off the roof, but I still wouldn't speak to him. So he stole me a saucer of milk and swore he would make sure Old Man didn't kill me, too. He liked me a lot better than the other cat, he said, because I was clever. Anyway, Old Man killed the other cat doing magic he would not be able to work again without a certain special powder. Besides, the other cat was black and did not look as interesting as me.

After Boy had told me a lot of things like this, I put my nose to his nose, and we were friends again. We made a conspiracy— that was what Boy called it—and swore to defeat Old Man and escape somehow. But we could not find out how to do it. We thought and thought. In the end I stopped growing because of the strain and worry. Boy said no, it was because I was full grown.

I said, "Why, in that case, are *you* still growing? You're already more than ten times my size. You're nearly as big as Old Man!"

"I know," said Boy. "You're an elegant little cat. I don't think

I shall be elegant until I'm six feet tall, and maybe not even then. I'm so clumsy. *And* so hungry!"

Poor Boy. He did grow so, around then. He did not seem to know his own size from one day to the next. When he rolled over in the cupboard, he either squashed me or burst out into the hallway. I had to scratch him quite hard, several nights, or he would have smothered me. And he kept knocking things over when he was awake. He spilled the milk jug—which I didn't mind at all—and he kicked Old Man's magic tripod by accident and smashed six jars of smelly stuff. Old Man cursed and called Boy a fool, worse than ever. And I think Boy really was stupid then, because he was so hungry. Old Man was too mean to give him more to eat. Boy ate my food, so I was hungry, too. He said he couldn't help it.

I went on the roof and caught pigeons. Boy roasted them over the gaslight at night when Old Man was asleep. Delicious. But the bones made me sick in the corner. We hid the feathers in the cupboard, and after I had caught a great many pigeons, night after night, the cupboard began to get warm. Boy began to get his mind back. But he still grew, and he was still hungry. By the time I had stopped growing for a year, Boy was so big his breeches went right up his legs and his legs went all hairy. Old Man couldn't hit him anymore then, because Boy just put out a long, long arm and held Old Man off.

"I need more clothes," he told Old Man.

Old Man grumbled and protested, but at last he said, "Oh, all right, you damn scarecrow. I'll see what I can do." He went unwillingly down into the cellar and heaved up one of the flagstones there. He wouldn't let me look in the hole, but I know that what was under that flagstone was Old Man's collection of all the rings and shiny stones that came from nowhere when I sat in the five-pointed star. I saw Old Man take some chinking things out. Then he slammed down the stone and went away upstairs, not noticing that one shiny thing had spilled out and gone rolling across the floor. It was a little golden ball. It was fun. I chased it for hours. I patted it and it rolled, and I pounced, and it ran away all around the cellar. Then it spoiled the fun by rolling down a crack between two flagstones and getting lost. Then I found I was shut in the cellar and had to make a great noise to be let out.

That reminds me: does your house have balls in it? Then buy me one tomorrow. Until then a piece of paper on some string will do.

Where was I? Oh, yes. Someone smelling of mildew came and let me out. I nearly didn't know Boy at first. He had a red coat and white breeches and long black boots on, all rather too big for him. He said it was an old soldier's uniform Old Man had picked up cheap, and how did I get shut in the cellar?

I sat around his neck and told him about the flagstone where Old Man kept his shinies. Boy was *very* interested. "That would buy an awful lot of food," he said. He was still hungry. "We'll take it with us when we escape. Let's try escaping next time he works magic."

So that night we made a proper plan at last. We decided to summon a Good Spirit, instead of the hateful things Old Man always fetched. "There must be *some* good ones," Boy said. But since we didn't know enough to summon a good one on our own, we had to make Old Man do it for us somehow.

We did it the very next day. I played up wonderfully. As soon as Old Man started to draw on the cellar floor, I ran away, so that Old Man would not suspect us. I dug my claws hard into Boy's coat when he caught me, so that Old Man could hardly pull me loose. And I scratched Old Man, very badly, so that there was blood when he put me inside the five-pointed star. Then I sat there, humped and sulky, and it was Boy's turn.

Boy did rather well, too. At first he was just the usual kind of clumsy and kicked some black powder into some red powder while they were putting it out in heaps, and the cellar filled with white soot. It was hard not to sneeze too soon, but I managed not to. I managed to hold the sneeze off until Old Man had done swearing at Boy and begun on the next bit, the mumbling. Then I sneezed—once. Boy promptly fell against the tripod, which dripped hot stuff on the spilled powder. The cellar filled with big purple bubbles. They drifted and shone and bobbed most enticingly. I would have loved to chase them, but I knew I mustn't, or we would spoil what we were doing. Old Man couldn't leave off his mumbling, because that would spoil the spell, but he glared at Boy through the bubbles. I sneezed again—two—to distract him. Old Man raised his stick and began on the chanting bit. And Boy pretended to trip and, as he did, he threw a fistful of powder he had ready into the gaslight.

Whup! it went.

Old Man jumped and glared and went on grimly chanting— he had to, you see, because you can't stop magic once you have started—and all the bubbles drifted to the floor and burst, *smicker, smicker,* very softly. As each one burst, there was a little tiny pink animal on the floor, running about and calling, "Oink, oink, oink!" in a small squeaky voice. That nearly distracted me, as well as Old Man. I stared out at them with longing. I would have given *worlds* to jump out of the star and chase those beasties. They looked so beautifully *eatable*. But I knew I mustn't try to come out of the star yet, so I shut my eyes and yawned to hold in the third sneeze and thought hard, hard, hard of a Good Thing. *Let a Good Thing come!* I thought. I thought as hard as you do when you see a saucer of milk held in the air above you, and you want them to put it on the floor—quick. Then I gave my third sneeze.

That reminds me. Milk? Yes, please, or I won't be able to tell you any more.

Thank you. Keep your knee steady. You may stroke me if you wish. Where was I?

Right. When I opened my eyes, all the delicious beasties had vanished and the light burned sort of dingily. Old Man was beating Boy over the head with a stick. He could do that for once, because Boy was crouched by the wall laughing until his face ran tears. "Pigs!" he said. "Tiny little pigs! Oh, oh, oh!"

"I'll pig *you*!" Old Man screamed. "You spoiled my spell! Look at the pentangle—there's nothing there at all!"

But there was. I could feel the new Thing inside me. It wasn't hateful at all, but it felt lost and a bit feeble. It was too scared to say or do anything or even let me move, until Old Man crossly broke the pentangle and stumped away upstairs.

Boy stood rubbing his head. "Pity it didn't work, Brindle," he said. "But wasn't it worth it just for those pigs?"

"Master," the Good Thing said with my mouth, "Master, how can I serve you, bound as I am?"

Boy stared, and his face went odd colors. I always wonder how you humans manage that. "Good Lord!" he said. "Did we do it after all? Or is it a demon?"

"I don't think I'm a demon," Good Thing said doubtfully. "I may be some kind of spirit. I'm not sure."

"Can't you get out of me?" I said to it in my head.

"No. Our Master would not be able to hear me if I did," it told me.

"Bother you then!" I said, and started to wash.

"You can serve me, anyway, whatever you are," Boy said to Good Thing. "Get me some food."

"Yes, Master," it made me say, and obeyed at once. I had just reached that stage of washing where you have one foot high in the air. I fell over. It was most annoying. Next minute I was rolling about in a huge warm room full of people cooking things. A kitchen, Boy said it was later. It smelled marvelous. . . . I hardly minded at all when Good Thing made me leap up and snatch a roast leg of mutton from the nearest table. But I did

mind—a lot—when two men in white hats rushed at me shouting, *"Damn cat!"*

Good Thing didn't know what to do about that at all, and it
nearly got us caught. "Let *me* handle this!" I spat at it, and it
did. I told you, it was a bit feeble. I dived under a big dresser
where people couldn't reach me and crouched there right at the
back by the wall. It was a pity I had to leave the meat behind. It
smelled wonderful. But I had to leave it, or they'd have gone on
chasing me. "Now," I said, when my coat had settled flat again,
"you tell me what you want me to take and I'll take it properly
this time."

Good Thing agreed that might work better. We waited until
they'd all gone back to cooking and then slunk softly out into
the room again. And Good Thing had been thinking all this
time. It made me a sort of invisible sack. It was most peculiar.
No one could see the sack, not even me, and it didn't get in my
way at all. I just knew it was behind me, filling up with the food
I stole. Good Thing made me take stuff I'd never have dreamed
of eating myself, like cinnamon jelly and—yuk!—cucumber, as
well as good honest meat and venison pie and other reasonable
things.

Then we were suddenly back in the cellar, where Boy was
glumly clearing up. When he saw the food spilling out onto the
floor, his face lit up. Good Thing had been right. He loved the
jelly and even ate cucumber. For once in his life he really had
enough to eat. I helped him eat the venison pie, and we both
had strawberries and cream to finish with. I love those.

Which reminds me— Oh. Strawberries are out of season?
Never mind. I'll stay with you until they come back in. Rub my
stomach again.

I was heavy and kind of round after that meal. Good Thing
complained rather. "Well, get out of me then, and it won't
bother you," I said. I wanted to sleep.

"In a minute," it said. "Master, the cat tells me you want to escape, but I'm afraid I can't help you there."

Boy woke up in dismay. He was dropping off to sleep on the floor, being so full. "Why *not*?"

"Two reasons," Good Thing said apologetically. "First, there is a very strong spell on you, which confines you to this house, and it is beyond my power to break it. Second, there is an equally strong spell on me. You and the cat broke part of it, the part which confined me to a small golden ball, but I am still forced to stay in the house where the golden ball is. The only other place I can go is the house I . . . came from."

"Damn!" said Boy. "I did hope—"

"The spell that confines the cat is nothing like so strong," Good Thing said. "I could raise that for you."

"That's something at least! Do that," said Boy. He was a generous Boy. "And if you two could keep on fetching food, so that I can put my mind to something besides how hungry I am, then I might think of a way to break the spell on you and me."

I was a little annoyed. It seemed that we had got Good Thing just because the golden ball had escaped from Old Man, and not because of Boy's cleverness or my powers of thought. But though I knew the ball was down a crack just inside the place where Old Man usually drew his pentangle, I didn't mention it to Boy in case his feelings were hurt, too.

We had great good times for quite a long while after that, Boy, Good Thing, and I, and Old Man never suspected at all. He was away a lot around then, anyway. While he was away, there were always a jug of milk and a loaf that appeared magically every four days, but Boy and I would have half starved on that without Good Thing. Good Thing took me to the kitchen place every day at suppertime, and we came back with every kind of food in the invisible sack. When Good Thing was not around—it quite often went away in the night and left me in peace—I went out across the roofs. I led a lovely extra life on top of the town. I met other cats by moonlight, but they were never as clever as me. I found out all sorts of things and came and told them to Boy. He was always very wistful about not being able to go out himself, but he listened to everything. He was like that. He was my friend. And he was a great comfort to me when I had my first kittens. I didn't know what was happening to me. Boy guessed and he told me. Then he told me that we must hide the kittens or Old Man would know I had been able to go out. We were very secret and hid them in our cupboard in a nest of pigeon feathers.

I am good at having kittens. I'll show you presently. I always have three, one tabby, one ginger, and one mixed like me. I had three kittens then, and Old Man never knew, even though they were quite noisy sometimes, especially after I taught them how to play with Good Thing.

When Good Thing came out of me, I could see it quite well, though Boy never could. It was quite big outside me, up to Boy's shoulder, and frail and wafty, and it could float about at great speed. It enjoyed playing. I used to hunt it all round the house and leap on it, pretending to tear it to bits, and of course it would waft away between my paws. Boy used to guess where Good Thing was from my behavior and laugh at me hunting it. He laughed even more when my kittens were old enough to play hunting Good Thing, too.

By this time Boy was a fine, strong Boy, full of thoughts, and his soldier clothes were getting too short and tight. He asked Good Thing to get him some more clothes next time Old Man was away. So Good Thing and I went to another part of the mansion where the kitchen was. Boy said "house" was the wrong word for that place. He was right. It was big and grand. This time when we got there, we went sneaking at a run up a great stair covered with red carpet—or I went sneaking with

Good Thing inside me—and along more carpet to a large room with curtains all around the walls. The curtains had pictures that Good Thing said were lords and ladies hunting animals with birds and horses. I never knew that *birds* were any help to people.

There was a space between the curtains and the walls, and Good Thing sent me sneaking through that space, around the room. There were people in the room. I peeped at them through a crack in the curtains.

There was a very fine Man there, almost as tall and fine as my Boy, but much older. With him were two of the ones in white hats from the kitchen. They held their hats in their hands, sorrowfully. With them was a Woman in long clothes, looking cross as Old Man.

"Yes indeed, sir, I saw this cat for myself, sir," the Woman said. "It stole a cake under my very eyes, sir."

"I swear to you, sir," one of the white hats said, "it appears every evening and vanishes like magic with every kind of food."

"It *is* magic, that's why," said the other white hat.

"Then we had better take steps to see where it comes from," the fine Man said. "If I give you this—"

Good Thing wouldn't let me stay to hear more. We ran on. "Oh, dear!" Good Thing said in my head as we ran. "We'll have to be very careful after this!" We came to a room that was white and gold, with mirrors. Good Thing wouldn't let me watch myself in the mirrors. The white-and-gold walls were all cupboards filled with clothes hanging or lying inside. We stuffed the invisible sack as full as it would hold with clothes from the cupboards, so that we would not need to go back. For once it felt heavy. I was glad to get back to Boy waiting in Old Man's book room.

"Great Scott!" said Boy as the fine coats, good boots, silk shirts, cravats, and smooth trousers tumbled out onto the floor. "I can't wear these! These are fit for a king! The Old Man would be bound to notice." But he could not resist trying some of them on, all the same. Good Thing told me he looked good. I thought Boy looked far finer than the Man they belonged to.

After this, Boy became very curious about the mansion where the clothes and the food came from. He made me describe everything. Then he asked Good Thing, "Are there books in this mansion, too?"

"And pictures and jewels," Good Thing said through me. "What does Master wish me to fetch? There is a golden harp, a musical box like a bird, a—"

"Just books," said Boy. "I need to learn. I'm still so ignorant."

Good Thing always obeyed Boy. The next night, instead of going to the kitchen, Good Thing took me to a vast room with a round ceiling held up by freckled pillars, where the walls were lined with books in shelves. Good Thing had one of its helpless turns there. "Which do you think our Master wants?" it asked me feebly.

"I don't know," I said. "I'm only a cat. Let's just take all we can carry. I want to get back to my kittens."

So we took everything out of one shelf, and it was not right. Boy said he did not need twenty-four copies of the Bible: one was enough. The same went for Shakespeare. And he could not read Greek, he said. I spat. But we gathered up all the books except two and went back.

We had just spilled all the books onto the floor of the room with the freckled pillars when the big door burst open. The Man came striding in, with a crowd of others. "There's the cat now!" they all cried out.

Good Thing had me snatch another book at random, and we went.

"And I daren't go back for a while, Master," Good Thing said to Boy.

I saw to my kittens; then I went out hunting. I fed Boy for the next few days—when he remembered to eat, that was. I stole a leg of lamb from an inn, a string of sausages from the butcher down the road, and a loaf and some buns from the baker. The kittens ate most of it. Boy was reading. He sat in his fine clothes, and he read, the Bible first, then Shakespeare, and then the book of history Good Thing had me snatch. He said he was educating himself. It was as if he were asleep. When Old Man suddenly came back, I had to dig all my claws into Boy to make him notice.

Old Man looked grumpily around everywhere to make sure everything was in order. He was always suspicious. I was scared. I made Good Thing stay with the kittens in the cupboard and hid the remains of the sausages in there with them. Boy was all dreamy, but he sat on the book of history to hide it. Old Man looked at him, hard. I was scared again. Surely Old Man would notice that Boy's red coat was of fine warm cloth and that there was a silk shirt underneath? But Old Man said, "Stupid as ever, I see," and grumped out of the house again.

Talking of sausages, when do you eat? Soon? Good. Now, go on stroking.

The next day Old Man was still away. Boy said, "Those were wonderful books. I must have *more*. I wish I didn't have to trust a cat and a spirit to steal them. Isn't there *any* way I can go and choose books for myself?"

Good Thing drifted about the house, thinking. At last it got into me and said, "There is no way I can take you to the mansion bodily, Master. But if you can go into a trance, I can take you there in spirit. Would that do?"

"Perfectly!" said Boy.

"Oh, no," I said. "If you do, I'm coming, too. I don't trust you on your own with my Boy, Good Thing. You might go feeble and lose him."

"I will *not*!" said Good Thing. "But you may come if you wish. And we will wait till the middle of the night, please. We don't want you to be seen again."

Around midnight Boy cheerfully went into a trance. Usually he hated it when Old Man made him do it. And we went to the mansion again, all three of us. It was very odd. I could see Boy there the way I could see Good Thing, like a big, flimsy cloud. As soon as we were there, Boy was so astonished by the grandeur of it that he insisted on drifting all around it, upstairs and down, to see as much as he could. I was scared. Not everyone was asleep. There were gaslights or candles burning in most of the corridors, and someone could easily have seen me. But I stuck close to Boy because I was afraid Good Thing would lose him.

It was not easy to stay close. They could go through doors without opening them. When they went through one door upstairs, I had to jump up and work the handle in order to follow Boy inside. It was a pretty room. The quilt on the bed was a cat's dream of comfort. I jumped up and paddled on it, while Boy and Good Thing hovered to look at the person asleep there. She was lit up by the nightlight beside the bed.

"What a *lovely* girl!" I felt Boy think. "She must be a princess."

She sat up at that. I think it was because of me treading on her stomach. I went tumbling way backward, which annoyed me a good deal. She stared. I glowered and wondered whether to spit. "Oh!" she said. "You're that magic cat my father wants to catch. Come here, puss. I promise I won't let him hurt you." She held out her hand. She was nice. She knew how to stroke a cat, just like you. I let her stroke me and talk to me, and I was just curling up to enjoy a rest on her beautiful quilt when a huge Woman sprang up from a bed on the other side of the room.

"Were you calling, my lady?" she asked. Then she saw me.

She screamed. She ran to a rope hanging in one corner and heaved at it, screaming, *"That cat's back!"*

"Run!" Good Thing said to me. "I'll look after Boy."

So I ran. I have never run like that in my life, before or since. It felt as if everyone in the mansion was after me. Luckily for me, I knew my way around quite well by then. I ran upstairs and I ran down, and people clattered after me, shouting. I dived under someone's hand and dodged through a crooked cupboard place, and at last I found myself behind the curtains in the Man's room. He ran in and out. Other people ran in and out, but the Princess really had done something to help me somehow and not one of them thought of looking behind those curtains.

After a bit I heard the Princess in that room, too. "But it's a *nice* cat, Father—really sweet. I can't think why you're making all this fuss about it!" Then there was a sort of grating sound. I smelled the smallest whiff of fresh air. Bless her, she had opened the Man's window for me.

I got out of it as soon as the room was empty. I climbed down onto grass. I ran again. I knew just the way I should go. Cats do, you know, particularly when they have kittens waiting for them. I was dead tired when I got to Old Man's house. It was right on the other side of town. As I scrambled through the skylight in the roof, I was almost too tired to move. But I was dead worried about my kittens and about Boy, too. It was morning by then.

My kittens were fine, but Boy was still lying on the floor of the book room in a trance, cold as ice. And as if that were not enough, keys grated in the locks and Old Man came back. All I could think to do was to lie around Boy's neck to warm him.

Old Man came and kicked Boy. "Lazy lump!" he said. "Anyone would think you were in a trance!" I couldn't think what to do. I got up and hurried about, mewing for milk, to distract Old Man. He wasn't distracted. Looking gleefully at Boy, he carefully put a jar of black powder away in his cupboard and locked it. Then he sat down and looked at one of his books, not bothering with me at all. He kept looking across at Boy.

My kittens distracted Old Man by having a fight in the cupboard about the last of the sausages. Old Man heard it and leaped up. "Scrambling and squeaking!" he said. "Mice! Could even be rats by the noise. Damn cat! Don't you ever do your job?" He hit at me with his stick.

I tried to run. Oh, I was tired! I made for the stairs, to take us both away from Boy and my kittens, and Old Man caught me by my tail halfway up. I was that tired. . . . I was forced to bite him quite hard and scratch his face. He dropped me with a thump, so he probably did not hear the even louder thump from the book room. I did. I ran back there.

Boy was sitting up, shivering. There was a pile of books beside him.

"Good Thing!" I said. "That was stupid!"

"Sorry," said Good Thing. "He would insist on bringing them." The books vanished into the invisible sack just as Old Man stormed in.

He ranted and grumbled at Boy for laziness and for feeding me so that I didn't catch mice, and he made Boy set mousetraps. Then he stormed off to the cellar.

"Why didn't you come back sooner?" I said to Boy.

"It was too marvelous being somewhere that wasn't this house," Boy said. He was all dreamy with it. He didn't even read his new books. He paced about. So did I. I realized that my kittens were not safe from Old Man. And if he found them, he would realize that I could get out of the house. Maybe he would kill me like the cat before. I was scared. I wished Boy would be scared, too. I wished Good Thing would show some sense. But Good Thing was only thinking of pleasing Boy.

"Don't let him go into a trance again," I said. "Old Man will know."

"But I *have* to!" Boy shouted. "I'm *sick* of this house!" Then he calmed down and thought. "I know," he said to Good Thing. "Fetch the Princess here."

Good Thing got into me and bleated that this wasn't wise now that Old Man was back. I said so, too. But Boy wouldn't listen. He had to have Princess. Or else he would go into a trance and see her that way. I understood then. Boy wanted kittens. Very little will stop boys or cats when they do.

So we gave in. When Old Man was asleep and snoring, Boy dressed himself in the middle of the night in the Man's finest clothes and looked fine as fine. He even washed in horrible cold water, in spite of all I said. Then Good Thing went to the mansion.

Instants later the Princess was lying asleep on the floor of the book room. "Oh," Boy said sorrowfully, "what a shame to wake her!" But he woke her up all the same.

She rubbed her eyes and stared at him. "Who are you, sir?"

Boy said, "Oh, Princess—"

She said, "I think you've made a mistake, sir. I'm not a princess. Are you a prince?"

Boy explained who he was and all about himself, and she explained that her father was a rich magician. She was a disappointment to him, she said, because she could hardly do any magic and was not very clever. But Boy still called her Princess. She said she would call him Orange because of his hair. She may not have been clever, but she was nice. I sat on her knee and purred. She stroked me and talked to Boy for the whole night, until it began to get light. They did nothing but talk. I said to Good Thing that it was a funny way to have kittens. Good Thing was not happy. Princess did not understand about Good Thing. Boy gave up trying to explain. Good Thing drifted about, sulking.

When it was really light, Princess said she must go back. Boy agreed, but they put it off and kept talking. That was when I had my good idea. I went to the cupboard and fetched out my kittens, one by one, and I put them into Princess's lap.

"Oh!" she said. "What beauties!"

"Tell her she's to keep them and look after them," I said to Boy.

He told her, and she said, "Brindle can't *mean* it! It seems such a sacrifice. Tell her it's sweet of her, but I *can't.*"

"Make her take them," I said. "Tell her they're a present from you, if it makes her happier. Tell her they're a sign that she'll see you again. Tell her *anything,* but make her take them!"

So Boy told her, and Princess agreed. She gathered the tabby and the ginger and the mixed kitten into her hands, and Good Thing took her and the kittens away. We stood staring at the place where she had been, Boy and I. Things felt empty, but I was pleased. My kittens were safe from Old Man, and Princess had kittens now, which ought to have pleased Boy, even if they were mine and not his. I did not understand why he looked so sad.

Old Man was standing in the doorway behind us. We had not heard him getting up. He glared at the fine way Boy was dressed. "How did you come by those clothes?"

"I did a spell," Boy said airily. Well, it was true in a way. Boy's mood changed when he realized how clever we had been. He said, "And Brindle got rid of the mice," and laughed.

Old Man was always annoyed when Boy laughed. "Funny, is it?" he snarled. "For that, you can go down to the cellar, you and your finery, and stay there till I tell you to come out." And he put one of his spells on Boy, so that Boy had to go. Old Man locked the cellar door on him. Then he turned back, rubbing his hands and laughing, too. "Last laugh's mine!" he said. "I *thought* he knew more than he let on, but there's no harm done. I've still got him!" He went and looked in almanacs and horoscopes and chuckled more. Boy was eighteen that day. Old Man began looking up spells, lots of them, from the bad black books that even he rarely touched.

"Brindle," said Good Thing, "I am afraid. Do one thing for me."

"Leave a cat in peace!" I said. "I need to sleep."

Good Thing said, "Boy will soon be dead and I will be shut out forever unless you help."

"But my kittens are safe," I said, and I curled up in the cupboard.

"They will not be safe," said Good Thing, "unless you do this for me."

"Do what for you?" I said. I was scared again, but I stretched as if I didn't care. I do *not* like to be bullied. You should remember that.

"Go to the cellar in my invisible sack and tell Boy where the golden ball is," Good Thing said. "Tell him to fetch it out of the floor and give it to you."

I stretched again and strolled past Old Man. His face was scratched all over, I was glad to see, but he was collecting things to work spells with now. I strolled quite fast to the cellar door. There Good Thing scooped me up and went inside, in near dark. Boy was sitting against the wall.

"Nice of you to come," he said. "Will Good Thing fetch Princess again tonight?" He did not think there was any danger. He was used to Old Man behaving like this. But I thought of my kittens. I showed him the place where the golden ball had got lost down the crack. I could see it shining down there. It took me ages to persuade Boy to dig it out, and even then he only worked at it idly, thinking of Princess. He could only get at it with one little finger, which made it almost too difficult for him to bother.

I heard Old Man coming downstairs. I am ashamed to say

that I bit Boy, quite hard, on the thumb of the hand he was digging with. He went *"Ow!"* and jerked, and the ball flew rolling
into a corner. I raced after it.

"Put it in your mouth. Hide it!" said Good Thing.

I did. It was hard not to swallow it. Then, when I didn't swallow, it was hard not to spit it out. Cats are made to do one or
the other. I had to pretend it was a piece of meat I was taking to
my kittens. I sat in the corner, in the dark, while Old Man came
in and locked the door and lit the tripod lamp.

"If you need Brindle," Boy said, sulkily sucking his hand, *"you*
can look for her. She bit me."

"This doesn't need a cat," Old Man said. Boy and I were both
astonished. "It just needs *you*," he told Boy. "This is the life
transfer spell I was trying on the black cat. This time I know
how to get it right."

"But you said you couldn't do it without a special powder!"
Boy said.

Old Man giggled. "What do you think I've been away looking
for all this year?" he asked. "I've got a whole jar of it! With it, I
shall put myself into your body and you into my body, and then
I shall kill this old body off. I won't need it or you after that. I
shall be young and handsome, and I shall live for years. Stand
up. Get into the pentangle."

"Blowed if I shall!" said Boy.

But Old Man did spells and made him. It took a long time because Boy resisted even harder than I usually did and shouted
spells back. In the end Old Man cast a spell that made Boy stand
still and drew the five-pointed star around him, not in the usual
place.

"I shall kill my old body with you inside it rather slowly for
that," he said to Boy. Then he drew another star, a short way
off. "This is for my bride," he said, giggling again. "I took her
into my power ten years ago, and by now she'll be a lovely

young woman." Then he drew a third star, overlapping Boy's, for himself, and stood in it chuckling. "Let it start!" he cried out, and threw the strong, smelly black powder on the tripod. Everything went green-dark. When the green went, Princess was standing in the empty star.

"Oh, it's *you*!" she and Boy both said.

"Aha!" said Old Man. "Hee-hee! So you and she *know* one another, do you? How you did it, boy, I won't inquire, but it makes things much easier for me." He began on his chanting.

"Give the golden ball to Princess," Good Thing said to me. "Hurry. Make Boy tell her to swallow it."

I ran across to Princess and spit the golden ball into her star. She pulled her skirt back from it.

"Brindle wants you to swallow it," Boy said. "I think it's important."

People are peculiar. Princess must have known it was very important, but she said faintly, "I can't! Not something that's been in a cat's *mouth*!"

Old Man saw the golden ball. He glared, still chanting, and raised his stick. The ball floated up and came toward him. Princess gave a last despairing snatch and caught it, just in time. She put it in her mouth.

"Ah! Back again!" said Good Thing.

Princess swallowed. She changed. She had been nice before but sort of stupid. Now she was nice and as clever as Boy. "You toad!" she said to Old Man. "That was part of my soul! You took it, didn't you?"

Old Man raised his stick again. Princess held up both hands. Magic raged, strong enough to make my fur stand up, and Old Man did not seem to be able to do much at first. It was interesting. Princess had magic, too, only I think it had all gone into Good Thing. But not quite enough. She started to lose. "Help me!" she said to Boy.

Boy started to say a spell, but at that moment the door of the cellar burst open, and half the wall fell in with it. The Man rushed in with a crowd of others.

"Father!" said Princess. "Thank goodness!"

"Are you all right?" said the Man. "We traced you through those kittens. What are you trying to do here, Old Man? The life transfer, is it? Well, that's enough of *that*!" The Man made signs that stood my coat up on end again.

Old Man screamed. I could tell he was dying. The spell had somehow turned back on him. He was withering and shrinking and getting older and older. Boy jumped out of his star and ran to Princess. They both looked very happy. Old Man snarled at them, but he could do nothing but round on me. Everyone does that. They all kick the cat when they can't kick a person. "So you had *kittens*!" he screamed. "This is all your fault, cat! For that, you shall have kittens to drown for the next thousand years!"

"I soften that curse!" the Man shouted.

Then everything went away, and I was not in the town I knew anymore. I have been wandering about, all these years, ever since. Old Man's curse means that I am good at having kittens. It is not a bad curse because the Man has softened it. Old Man meant my kittens to be drowned every time. But instead, if I can find an understanding person—like you—who will listen to my story, then my kittens will have good homes, and so will I for a time. You won't mind. They'll be beautiful kittens. They always are. You'll see very soon now. After supper.

NAD AND
DAN ADN QUAFFY

She had struggled rather as a writer until she got her word processor. Or not exactly *struggled,* she thought, frowning at her screen and flipping the cursor back to correct *adn* to *and.* For some reason, she always garbled the word *and.* It was always *adn* or *nad; dna* or *nda* was less frequent, but all of them appeared far oftener than the right way. She had only started to make this mistake after she gave up her typewriter, and she felt it was a small price to pay.

For years she had written what seemed to her the most stirring sort of novels, about lonely aliens among humans, or lonely humans among aliens, or sometimes both kinds lonely in an unkind world, all without ever quite hitting the response from readers she felt she was worth. Then came her divorce, which left her with custody of her son, Daniel, then thirteen. That probably provided an impetus of some sort in itself, for Danny was probably the most critical boy alive.

"Mum!" he would say. "I wish you'd give *up* that lonely-heart alien stuff! Can't you write about something decent for a change?" Or, staring at her best efforts at cookery, he said, "I can't be expected to eat *this!*" After which he had taken over cooking himself: they now lived on chili con carne and stir-fry. For as Danny said, "A man can't be expected to learn more than one dish a year." At the moment, being nearly fifteen, Danny was teaching himself curry. Their nice Highgate house reeked of burned garam masala most of the time.

But the real impetus had come when she found Danny in her workroom sternly plaiting the letters of her old typewriter into metal braid. "I've had this old thing!" he said when she tore him away with fury and cursings. "So have you. It's out of the ark. Now you'll have to get a word processor."

"But I don't know how to work the things!" she had wailed.

"That doesn't matter. I do. I'll work it for you," he replied inexorably. "And I'll tell you what one to buy, too, or you'll only waste money."

He did so. The components were duly delivered and installed, and Daniel proceeded to instruct his mother in how to work as much of them as—as he rather blightingly said—her feeble brain would hold. "There," he said. "Now write something worth reading for a change." And he left her sitting in front of it all.

When she thought about it, she was rather ashamed of the fact that her knowledge of the thing had not progressed one whit beyond those first instructions Danny had given her. She had to call on her son to work the printout, to recall most of the files, and to get her out of any but the most simple difficulty. On several occasions—as when Danny had been on a school trip to Paris or away with his school cricket team—she had had to tell her publisher all manner of lies to account for the fact that there would be no copy of anything until Danny got back. But the advantages far outweighed these difficulties, or at least she knew they did *now*.

That first day had been a nightmare. She had felt lost and foolish and weak. She had begun, not having anything else in mind, on another installment of lonely aliens. And everything kept going wrong. She had to call Danny in ten times in the first hour, and then ten times after lunch, and then again when, for some reason, the machine produced what she had written of Chapter I as a list, one word to a line. Even Danny took most of the rest of the day to sort out what she had done to get that.

After that he hovered over her solicitously, bringing her mugs of black coffee, until, somewhere around nine in the evening, she realized she was in double bondage, first to a machine and then to her own son.

"Go away!" she told him. "Out of my sight! I'm going to learn to do this for myself or die in the attempt!"

Danny gave her bared teeth a startled look and fled.

By this time she had been sitting in front of board and screen for nearly ten hours. It seemed to her that her threat to die in the attempt was no idle one. She felt like death. Her back ached, and so did her head. Her eyes felt like running blisters. She had cramp in both hands and one foot asleep. In addition, her mouth was foul with too much coffee and Danny's chili con carne. The little green letters on the screen kept retreating behind the glass to the distant end of a long, long tunnel. "I *will* do this!" she told herself fiercely. "I am an intelligent adult—probably even a genius—and I will *not* be dominated by a mere machine!"

And she typed all over again:

CHAPTER ONE

The Captain had been at board and screen ever since
jump—a total of ten hours. Her hands shook with
weariness, making it an effort to hold them steady
on her switches. Her head was muzzy, her mouth
foul with nutrient concentrates. But since the mutiny,
it was sit double watches or fail to bring the starship
Candida safely through the intricate system of
Meld. . . .

At this point she began to get a strange sense of power. She *was* dominating this damned machine, even though she was doing it only by exploiting her own sensations. Also, she was becoming interested in what might be going to happen to the starship *Candida,* not to speak of the reasons that had led up to the mutiny aboard her. She continued writing furiously until long after midnight. When she stopped at last, she had to pry her legs loose from her chair.

"*That's* more like it, Mum!" Danny said the next morning, reading it as it came from the printer.

He was, as usual, right. *Starship Candida* was the book that made the name of F. C. Stone. It won prizes. It sold in resorts and newsagents all over the world. It was, reviewers said, equally remarkable for its insight into the Captain's character as for the intricate personal relationships leading to the mutiny. Much was spoken about the tender and peculiar relationships between the sexes. This last made F. C. Stone grin rather. All she had done was to revenge herself on Danny by reversing the way things were between them. In the book the Captain was all-powerful and dominating and complained a lot about the food. The Mate had a hypnotically induced mind-set that caused him to bleat for assistance at the first sign of trouble.

Her next book, *The Mutineers,* was an even greater success. For this one, F. C. Stone extended the intricate personal relationships to the wider field of galactic politics. She discovered she reveled in politics. Provided she was making up the politics herself, there seemed no limit to how intricate she could make them.

Since then she had, well, *not* stuck to a formula—she was much more artfully various than that—but as she said and Danny agreed, there was no point in leaving a winning game. Though she did not go back to starship *Candida,* she stayed with that universe and its intricate politics. There were aliens in it, too, which she always enjoyed. And she kept mostly out in space, so that she could continue to describe pilots astronauting at the controls of a word processor. Sooner or later in most of her books, someone, human or alien, would have sat long hours before the screen until dazed with staring, aching in the back, itching in the nose—for the burning of Asian spices in the kitchen tended to give her hay fever—and with cramped hands, this pilot would be forced to maneuver arduously through jump. This part always, or nearly always, got written when F. C. Stone was unable to resist staying up late to finish the chapter.

Danny continued to monitor his mother. He was proud of what he had made her do. In holidays and around the edges of school, he hung over her shoulder and brought her continual mugs of strong black coffee. This beverage began to appear in the books, too. The mutineer humans drank *gav,* while their law-abiding enemies quaffed *chvi.* Spacer aliens staggered from their nav-couches to gulp down *kivay,* and the mystics of Meld used *xfy* to induce an altered state of consciousness, although this was not generally spotted as being the same substance. And it was all immensely popular.

It was all due to the word processor, she thought, giving the nearest component a friendly pat as she leaned toward the screen again. The latest mug of cooling *kivay* sat beside her. Her nose was, as usual, tickled by burned ginger or something. Her back was beginning to ache, or, more truthfully, her behind was. She ought to get a more comfortable chair, but she was too fond of this old one. Anyway, the latest book was the thing. For this one, she had at last gone back to starship *Candida.* There had been a lot of pressure from her fans. And her publisher thought there was enough material in their suggestions, combined with F. C. Stone's own ideas, to make a trilogy. So she had decided to start in the way she knew would get her going. She typed:

Jump. Time nad the world stretched dna went out.
Back. The Captain had sat at her boards for four ob-
jective days—four subjective minutes or four subjec-

tive centuries. Her head ached, gums adn all. She
cursed. Hands trembling on controls, she struggled to
get her fix on this system's star.

Now what had some vastly learned reader suggested about this
system's star? It had some kind of variability, but that was all she
could remember. Damn. All her notes for it were in that file
Danny had set up for her. He was at school. But he had written
down for her how to recall it. She fumbled around for his piece
of paper—it had worked halfway under a black box whose name
and function she never could learn—and took a swig of luke-
warm *xfy* while she studied what to do. It looked quite simple.
She took another sip of *gav*. Store the new book. Careful not to
cancel this morning's work. There. Screen blank. Now type in
this lot, followed by *Candida 2*. Then—
    A clear childish voice spoke. "This is Candida Two, Candy," it
said. "Candida One, I need your confirmation."
    It was no voice F. C. Stone knew, and it seemed to come from
the screen. Her eyes turned to the mug of *kivay*. Perhaps she was
in a state of altered consciousness.
    "Candida One!" the voice said impatiently. "Confirm that
you are conscious. I will wait ten seconds and then begin lifesav-
ing procedures. Ten, nine, eight . . ."
    This sounded serious. Coffee poisoning, thought F. C. Stone.
I shall change to carrot juice or cocoa.
    ". . . seven, six, five," counted the childish voice, "four,
three . . ."
    I'd better say something, thought F. C. Stone. How absurd.
Weakly she said, "Do stop counting. It makes me nervous."
    "*Are* you Candida One?" demanded the voice. "The voice
pattern does not quite tally. Please say something else for comparison with my records."
    Why should I? thought F. C. Stone. But it was fairly clear that

if she stayed silent, the voice would start counting again and then, presumably, flood the room with the antidote for *xfy*.

No, no, this was ridiculous. There was no way a word processor could flood anyone's system with anything. Come to that, there was no way it could speak either—or was there? She must ask Danny. She was just letting her awe of the machine, and her basic ignorance, get on top of her. Let us be rational here, she thought. If she was not suffering from *gav* poisoning, or if, alternatively, the smell of charred turmeric at present flooding the house did not prove to have hallucinogenic properties, then she had worked too long and hard imagining things and was now unable to tell fantasy from reality . . . unless—what a *wonderful* thought!—Danny had, either for a joke or by accident, connected one of the black boxes to the radio and she was at this moment receiving its *Play for the Day*.

Her hand shot out to the radio beside her, which she kept for aural wallpaper during the duller part of her narratives, and switched it on. Click. "During this period Beethoven was having to contend with his increasing deafness—"

The childish voice cut in across this lecture. "This voice is not correct," it pronounced, putting paid to that theory. "It is the voice of a male. Males are forbidden access to any of my functions beyond basic navigational aids. Candida One, unless you reply confirming that you are present and conscious, I shall flood this ship with sedative gas ten seconds from now."

Then perhaps Danny has put a cassette in the radio as a joke, thought F. C. Stone. She turned off the radio and, for good measure, shook it. No, no cassette in there.

And the childish voice was at its counting again: ". . . six, five, four . . ."

Finding that her mouth was hanging open, F. C. Stone used it. "I know this is a practical joke," she said. "I don't know what it is you've done, Danny, but my God, I'll skin you when I get my hands on you!"

The countdown stopped. "Voice patterns are beginning to match," came the pronouncement, "though I do not understand your statement. Are you quite well, Candy?"

Fortified by the knowledge that this had to be a joke of Danny's, F. C. Stone snapped, "Yes, of course I am!" Very few people knew that the C. in F. C. Stone stood for Candida, and even fewer knew that she had, in her childhood, most shamingly been known as Candy. But Danny of course knew both these facts. "Stop this silly joke, Danny, and let me get back to work."

"Apologies," spoke the childish voice, "but who is Danny? There are only two humans on this ship. Is that statement addressed to the male servant beside you? He asks me to remind you that his name is Adny."

The joke was getting worse. Danny was having fun with her typos now. F. C. Stone was not sure she would ever forgive him for that. "And I suppose you're going to tell me we've just emerged in the Dna System and will be coming in to ladn at Nad," she said bitterly.

"Of course," said the voice.

F. C. Stone spent a moment in angry thought. Danny had to be using a program of some kind. She ought first to test this theory and then, if it was correct, find some way to disrupt the program and get some peace. "Give me your name," she said, "with visual confirmation."

"If you like," the voice responded. Had it sounded puzzled? Then Danny had thought of this. "I am Candida Two. I am your conscious-class computer modeled on your own brain." It sounded quite prideful, saying this. But, thought F. C. Stone, a small boy co-opted by a grand fifteen-year-old like Danny *would* sound prideful. "We are aboard the astroship *Partlett* M32/A401."

Motorways, thought F. C. Stone, but where did he get the name?

"Visual," said the voice. Blocks of words jumped onto the screen. They seemed to be in—Russian? Greek?—capitals.

It had to be a computer game of some kind, F. C. Stone thought. Now what would Danny least expect her to do? Easy. She plunged to the wall and turned the electricity off. Danny would not believe she would do that. He would think she was too much afraid of losing this morning's work, and maybe she would, but she could do it over again. As the blocks of print faded from the screen, she stumped off to the kitchen and made herself a cup of *xfy*—no, COFFEE!—and prowled around in there amid the smell of cauterized ginger while she drank it, with some idea of letting the system cool off thoroughly. She had a vague notion that this rendered a lost program even more lost. As far as she was concerned, this joke of Danny's couldn't be lost enough.

The trouble was that she was accustomed so to prowl whenever she was stuck in a sentence. As her annoyance faded, habit simply took over. Halfway through the mug of *quaffy*, she was already wondering whether to call the taste in the Captain's mouth merely *foul* or to use something more specific, like *chicken shit*. Five minutes later F. C. Stone mechanically made herself a second mug of *chofiy*—almost as mechanically noting that this seemed to be a wholly new word for the stuff and absently constructing a new kind of alien to drink it—and carried it through to her workroom to resume her day's stint. With her mind by then wholly upon the new solar system just entered by the starship *Candida*—there was no need to do whatever it was the learned fan wanted; after all, neither of them had *been* there and *she* was writing this book, not he—she switched the electicity back on and sat down.

Neat blocks of Greco-Cyrillic script jumped to her screen. "Candy!" said the childish voice. "Why don't you answer? I repeat. We are well inside the Dna System and coming up to jump."

F. C. Stone was startled enough to swallow a mouthful of scalding *c'phee* and barely notice what it was called. "Nonsense, Danny," she said, somewhat hoarsely. "Everyone knows you don't jump inside a solar system."

The script on the screen blinked a little. "His name is Adny," the voice said, sounding a little helpless. "If you do not remember that, or that microjumps are possible, then I see I must attend to what he has been telling me. Candy, it is possible that you have been overtaken by senility—"

"*Senility!*" howled F. C. Stone. Many murderous fates for Danny crowded through her mind.

"—and your male has been imploring me to ask you to authorize his use of functions Five through Nine to preserve this ship. Will you so authorize? Some action is urgent."

A certain curiosity emerged through F. C. Stone's anger. How far was Danny prepared to take his joke? How many possibilities had he allowed for? "I authorize," she said carefully, "his use of functions Five through *Eight* only." And let's see if he planned for that! she thought.

It seemed he had. A symbol of some kind now filled the screen, a complex curlicue the like of which F. C. Stone had never seen or imagined her equipment capable of producing. A wholly new voice spoke, male and vibrant. "I thank you," it said. "Function Eight will serve for now. This justifies my faith in you, Candida Three. I am now able to bypass the computer and talk to you direct. Please do not turn your power source off again. We must talk."

It was a golden voice, the voice, perhaps, of an actor, a voice that made F. C. Stone want to curl up and purr and maybe put her hair straight, even while she was deciding there was no way Danny could have made his rough and squawky baritone sound like this. Gods! He must have hired someone! She gave that boy far too much money. She took another swig of *ogvai* while she noted that the voice was definitely in some way connected to the symbol on the screen. The curlicue jumped and wavered in time to its words.

"What do you mean by calling me Candida Three?" she asked coldly.

"Because you are the exact analogue of my mistress, Candida One," the golden voice replied. "Her ship's computer is known as Candida Two. It therefore followed that when I had searched the universes and discovered you, I came to think of you as Candida Three. I have been studying you—most respectfully, of course—through this machine you use and the thoughts you set down on it, for two years now, and—"

"And Daniel has been reading other books besides mine," F. C. Stone interrupted. "Unfaithful brat!"

"I beg your pardon?" The symbol on the screen gave an agitated jump.

Score one to me! F. C. Stone thought. "My son," she said. "And we're talking parallel universes here, I take it?"

"We are." The golden voice sounded both cautious and bemused. "Forgive me if I don't quite follow you. You take the same sudden leaps of mind as my mistress, though I have come to believe that your mind is far more open than hers. She was born to a high place in the Matriarchy and is now one of the most powerful members of the High Coven—"

"Coven!" said F. C. Stone. "Whose book is this out of?"

There was a pause. The curlicue gave several agitated jumps. Then the golden voice said, "Look, please let me explain. I'm delaying jump as long as I can, but there really is only a very narrow window before I have to go or abort."

He sounded very pleading. Or perhaps *beguiling* was a better word, F. C. Stone thought, for that kind of voice. "All right," she said. "Get on with the program. But just tell me first what you mean when you say *mistress*, Danny."

"Adny," he said. "My name is Adny."

"Adny, then," said F. C. Stone. "*Mistress* has two meanings."

"Why, I suppose I mean both," he answered. "I was sold to Candy as a child, the way all men are in this universe. Men have almost no rights in the Matriarchy, and the Matriarchy is the chief power in our galaxy. I have been luckier than most, being sold to a mistress who is an adept of the High Coven. I have learned from her—"

F. C. Stone gave a slight exasperated sigh. For a moment there she had been uneasy. It had all seemed far more like a conversation than any program Danny could produce. But his actor friend seemed to have got back to his lines now. She shot forth another question. "So where is your mistress now?"

"Beside me, unconscious," was the reply.

"Senile?" said F. C. Stone.

"Believe me, they are liable to it," he said. "The forces they handle do seem to damage them, and it does seem to overtake them oftenest when they're out in space. But"—she could hear the smile in his voice—"I must confess that I was responsible for this one. It took me years of study before I could outwit her, but I did it."

"Congratulations, Adny," said F. C. Stone. "What do you want me to do about it? You're asking me to help you in your male backlash, is that it?"

"Yes, but you need do almost nothing," he replied. "Since you are the counterpart of Candida One, the computer is accepting you already. If you wish to help me, all I need is your voice authorizing Candida Two to allow me functions Nine and Ten. I can then tap my mistress's full power and navigate the ship to my rendezvous, whereupon I will cut this connection and cease interrupting you in your work."

"*What!*" said F. C. Stone. "You mean I don't get to navigate a word processor?"

"I don't understand," said Adny.

"Then you'd better!" said F. C. Stone. She was surprised at how strongly she felt. "Listen, Danny or Adny, or whoever you are! My whole career, my entire *success* as a writer, has been founded on the fact that I *enjoy,* more than anything else, sitting in front of this screen and pretending it's the controls of a starship. I enjoy the dazed feeling, I like the exhaustion, I don't mind getting cramp, and I even like drinking myself sick on *ogvai*! The only reason I haven't turned the machine off again is the chance that you're going to let me do it for real—or what feels like for real, I don't care which—and I'm not going to let that chance slip. You let me pilot my WP and I'll even authorize you to function Eleven afterward, if there is such a thing. Is that clear?"

"It is very clear, Great Lady," he said. There was that in his tone that suggested he was very used to yielding to demanding women, but could there have been triumph in it, too?

F. C. Stone was not sure of that tone, but she did not let it worry her. "Right," she said. "Brief me."

"Very well," he said, "though it may not be what you expect. We are about to make a microjump which in the normal way would bring us out above the spaceport but in this case is designed to bring us directly above the city of Nad and, hopefully, inside the Coven's defenses there. Other ships of my conspiracy should be materializing, too, hopefully at the same moment, so the jump must be made with utmost accuracy. I can broadcast you a simulacrum of *Partlett*'s controls, scaled down to correspond to your own keyboard. But you must depress the keys in exactly the order in which I highlight them. Can you do this?"

"Yes," said F. C. Stone. "But stop saying *hopefully,* or I shan't grant you any functions at all. The word shouldn't be used like that, and I detest sloppy English!"

"Yours to command," Adny said. She could hear the smile in his voice again. "Here are your controls."

The curlicue faded from the screen, to be replaced by a dia-grammatic image of F. C. Stone's own keyboard. It was quite recognizable, except to her dismay, an attempt had been made to repeat it three times over. The two outer representations of it were warped and blurred. "Gods!" said F. C. Stone. "How do I use this? There isn't room for it all."

"Hit HELP before you use the extra keys on the right and CAP before you use the ones on the left." Adny's voice reassured her. "Ready?"

She was. She took a hasty sip of cooling *qavv* to steady herself and hovered over her keyboard, prepared to enjoy herself as never before.

It was actually a bit of a letdown. Keys on her screen shone brighter green. Obedient to them, F. C. Stone found herself typing CAP *A, d,* HELP *N* and then HELP *N, a, D*. Some part of her mind suggested that this still looked like Danny's joke, while another part, more serious, suggested it might be overwork and perhaps she should see a doctor. But she refused to let either of these thoughts distract her and typed CAP *D, n,* HELP *A* in high excitement.

As she did so, she heard the computer's childish voice again. "Ready for jump. Candida One, are you sure of this? Your coor-dinates put us right on top of Nad, in considerable danger from our own defenses."

"Reassure her," Adny's voice said urgently.

Without having to think, F. C. Stone said soothingly, "It's all right, Candida Two. We have to test those defenses. Nad is under orders not to hurt us." And she thought, As to the man-ner born! I'd have made a good Matriarch!

"Understood," said the childish voice. "Jump as given, on the count of zero. Five, four, three"—F. C. Stone braced herself—"two, one, zero."

Did she feel a slight lurch? Was there a mild ripple of giddiness? She was almost sure not. A quick look around the work-room assured her that all was as usual.

"Jumping," said Candida Two. "There will be an interval of five subjective minutes."

"Why?" said F. C. Stone, like a disappointed child.

Adny's voice cut in hastily. "Standard for a microjump. Don't make her suspicious!"

"But I don't *feel* anything!" F. C. Stone complained in a whisper.

The keyboards vanished from the screen. "Nobody does," said Adny. "Computer's out of the circuit now. You can speak freely. There is no particular sensation connected with jump, though disorientation does occur if you try to move about."

"Damn!" said F. C. Stone. "I shall have to revise all my books!" An acute need to visit the toilet down the passage came upon her. She picked up her mug of *chphy* reflexively, thought better of that, and put it down again. Her mind dwelt on that toilet, its bowl stained from Danny's attempt, some years ago, to concoct an elixir of life, and its chain replaced by a string of cow bells. To take her mind off it, she said, "Tell me what you mean to do when you and the other ships come out over Nad. Does this start a revolution?"

"It's rather more complicated than that," said Adny. "Out of the twelve Male Lodges, there are only six prepared to rebel. Two of the remaining six are neutral traditionally and supported in this by the Minor Covens, but the Minor Covens are disaffected enough to ally with the Danai, who are a helium life-form and present a danger to all of us. The four loyal Lodges are supposed to align with the Old Coven, and on the whole they do, except for the Fifth Lodge, which has thrown in with the Mid-most Coven, who are against everyone else. Their situation is complicated by their concessions to the Traders, who are largely independent, save for overtures they seem to have made to the

Anders. The Anders—another life-form—have said they are *our* allies, but this flirting with the Traders makes us suspicious. So we decided on a bold ploy to test—"

"Stop!" said F. C. Stone. Much as she loved writing this kind of stuff, hearing someone talk like it made her head reel. "You mean, you've gone to all this trouble just for a test run?"

"It's more complicated than—" began Adny.

"No, I don't want to know!" said F. C. Stone. "Just tell me what happens if you fail."

"We can't fail," he replied. "If we do, the High Coven will crush the lot of us."

"Me, too?" F. C. Stone inquired anxiously.

"Possibly," said Adny. "They may not realize how I did this, but if they do, you can probably stop them by destroying your machine."

"Never!" said F. C. Stone. "I'd rather suffer—or, better still, win!"

A bell rang. The keyboard reappeared, elongated and bent, in her screen. "Emerged over Nad," the computer said. "Candy! What is this? I count sixteen other ships emerged, two Trader, four Ander, and the rest appear to be Matriarch. We jump back."

"Give me functions Nine and Ten!" Adny snapped.

"I authorize Adny—" said F. C. Stone.

"Oh, Candy!" the computer said reproachfully. "Why are you so good to that little creep? He's only a man."

"I authorize Adny in functions Nine and Ten," F. C. Stone almost shrieked. It was the only way she could think of to stop the unpleasant sensations which were suddenly manifesting, mostly in her head and stomach. It was as if surf were breaking through her in bubbles of pain. A tearing feeling across her shoulders made her think she was germinating claws there. And psychic attack or not, she knew she just had to get to that toilet.

"Acknowledged," the computer said glumly.

She leaped from her chair and ran. Behind her she heard claps of sound and booms that seemed to compress the air around her. Through them she heard Adny's voice issuing orders, but that was shortly overlaid by a high-pitched whistling, drilling through her ears even through the firmly shut toilet door.

But in the loo, as she was adjusting her dress, a certain sanity was restored to F. C. Stone. She looked at her own face in the mirror. It was encouragingly square and solid and as usual—give or take a sort of wildness about the eyes—and it topped the usual rather overweight body in its usual comfortably shapeless sweater. She raked her fingers through the graying frizz of her hair, thinking as she did so that she would make a very poor showing beside Adny of the golden voice. The action brought away two handfuls of loose hair. As always, she was shedding hair after a heavy session at the word processor—a fact she was accustomed to transfer to her aliens, who frequently shed feathers or fur during jump. Things were quite normal. She had simply been overworking and let Danny's joke get to her.

Or perhaps it was charred chili powder, she thought as she marched out into the passage again. Possibly due to its hallucinogenic nature, that damnable whistling was still going on, pure torture to her ears. From the midst of it she could hear Adny's voice. "Ned Coven, do we have your surrender, or do we attack again?"

I've had enough! thought F. C. Stone. She marched to her desk, where the screen was showing Adny's curlicue, pulsing to the beat of the beastly shrilling. "Stop this noise!" she commanded. "And give me a picture of *Partlett*'s flight deck." If you *can,* she thought, feeling for the moment every inch the captain of the starship *Candida.*

The whistling died to an almost bearable level. "I need function Eleven to give you vision," Adny said—irritably? casually?

or was it *too* casually? He was certainly overcasual when he
added, "It does exist, you know."

Give him what he wants and get rid of him, thought F. C.
Stone. "I authorize function Eleven then," she said.

"Oh!" said the computer, like a hurt child.

And there was a picture on the screen, greenish and jumping
and sleeting green lines, but fairly clear for all that. *Partlett*'s
controls, F. C. Stone noted absently, had fewer screens than she
expected—far fewer than she put in her books—but far more
ranks of square buttons and far, far too many dials for comfort,
all of them with a shabby, used look. But she was looking mostly
at the woman who seemed to be asleep in the padded swivel seat
in front of the controls. Mother naked, F. C. Stone was slightly
shocked to see, and not a mark or a wrinkle on her slender body
or on her thin and piquant face. Abruptly F. C. Stone remembered being quite proud of her looks when she was seventeen,
and this woman was herself at seventeen, only beyond even her
most idealized memories. Immense regret suffused F. C. Stone.

The whistling, blessedly, stopped. "Candy is really the same
age as you," Adny observed.

Her attention turned to him. His seat was humbler, a padded
swivel stool. Sitting on it was a small man with a long, nervy
face, the type of man who usually has tufts of hair growing in his
ears and below his eyes, as if to make up for the fact that such
men's hair always tends to be thin and fluffy on top. Adny's hair
was noticeably thin on top, but he had smoothed and curled it
to disguise the fact, and it was obvious that he had plucked and
shaved all other hair from his wrinkled little body; F. C. Stone
had no doubt of this, since he was naked, too. The contrast between his appearance and his voice was, to say the least of it,
startling.

Adny saw her look and grinned rather ruefully as he leaned
forward to hold a paper cup under some kind of tap below the

control panel. She realized he could see her, too. The contrast between herself and the sleeping beauty beside him made her feel almost as rueful as he looked. "Can you give me a picture of Nad and any damage there?" she asked, still clinging to her role as Captain. It seemed the only way to keep any dignity.

"Certainly," he said, running his finger down a row of the square buttons.

She found herself apparently staring down at a small town of old houses built up against the side of a hot stony hill—red roofs, boxlike white houses, courtyards shaded with trees. It was quite like a town in Spain or Italy, except that the shapes of the walls and the slant of the roofs were subtly different and wrong. It was the very smallness of the difference between this and towns she knew which, oddly enough, convinced F. C. Stone for once and for all that this place was no fake. She really was looking at a real town in a real world somewhere else entirely. There was a smoking, slaggy crater near the market square and another downhill below the town. That had destroyed a road. She had glimpses of the other spaceships, drifting about looking rather like hot-air balloons.

"Why is it such a small place?" she said.

"Because Nad is only a small outpost of the Matriarchy," Adny replied in his golden voice. The picture flipped back to show he had turned to face her on his stool, sipping steaming liquid from his paper cup. No doubt it was *kfa* or even *quphy*. He smiled through its steam in a way that must have beguiled the poor sleeping beauty repeatedly, and she found she was wishing he had turned out to be an alien instead. "I owe you great thanks on behalf of the Second Male Lodge," he said. "We now have the Nadlings where we want them. And since you have given me full control of this ship and access to all my ex-mistress's power, I can move on to the central worlds in strength and use her as a hostage there."

Hitler and Napoleon were both small men, F. C. Stone thought, with golden voices. It gave her a slight, cold frisson to think what she might have loosed on the unfortunate Matriarchy. "You gave me the impression that this *was* the central world," said F. C. Stone.

"Not in so many words," said Adny. "You don't think I'd be fool enough to move against the strength of the Matriarchy without getting hold of a conscious-class computer first, do you?"

F. C. Stone wished to say that yes, she did. People took that sort of desperate risk in her books all the time. It depressed her to find him such a cautious rebel. *And* he had cheated her, as well as his sleeping beauty, and no doubt he was all set to turn the whole works into a Patriarchy. It was a total waste of a morning.

Or was it? she wondered. A matriarchy where men were sold as slaves was right up her street. There was certainly a book in there. Perhaps she should simply be grateful and hope that Adny did not get too far.

"Tell me," she said, at which he looked up warily from his cup, "what is that stuff you're drinking? *Goffa? Xvay?*"

She was glad to see she had surprised him. "Only coffee," he said.